Had she found love only to lose it?

Beyke casually observed, "I had every intention of marrying Raf, but...the timing was wrong. Now I've been left high and dry."

Katrina asked cautiously, "Do you love him very much?"

Beyke shrugged. "Oh, I'll get over it. It's a pity he takes marriage so seriously—otherwise I might prize him loose from you." She made a delightful face and laughed.

Katrina forced a laugh, too, then asked politely, "Where do you live? Raf didn't say...."

"In Den Haag. You must come and visit. Raf knows the way. I haven't got a car yet, but Raf will drive me back."

The Hague was no great distance away, so why, Katrina fumed later, was Raf two hours getting there and back? And all she could do was wait in bed, alone....

When
May Follows

by

BETTY NEELS

Harlequin Books

TORONTO • LONDON • LOS ANGELES • AMSTERDAM
SYDNEY • HAMBURG • PARIS • STOCKHOLM • ATHENS • TOKYO

Original hardcover edition published in 1980
by Mills & Boon Limited

ISBN 0-373-02415-0

Harlequin edition published July 1981

Printed in U.S.A.

CHAPTER ONE

THE long low room gleamed in the firelight and the soft light from several lamps, giving a patina to the few pieces of well-polished yew and apple wood and glancing off the beams, blackened with age, which supported the ceiling. The room was full of people; the steady hum of talk and the frequent laughter witness to the success of the gathering.

The two men, latecomers, paused in the doorway to look around them and the elder of them, a short stout man with a fringe of grey hair surrounding a bald head, gave a rich chuckle. 'Dear Alice, she only gives two parties a year, you know, and everyone for miles around comes to one or both of them.'

He turned to look at his companion, a tall man with broad shoulders but lean nonetheless, elegantly turned out too in a superbly tailored suit, which, while not drawing attention to itself in any way, caused the discerning to realise that it had cost a great deal of money. He was a handsome man too, with a narrow face and a wide forehead, dark hair silvered with grey, an aquiline nose above a firm mouth, and heavily-lidded blue eyes.

He smiled now and said in a rather sleepy voice: 'It was good of you to bring me—I shall be delighted to meet Mrs Bennett.'

'And her daughters,' finished his companion, and waved to someone in the room. 'Here's Alice now.'

Mrs Bennett came towards them smiling; she was a small pretty woman in her mid-fifties but looking younger. She planted a kiss on the older man's cheek and said happily: 'Ben, how lovely!' Her eyes took in his companion. 'And you've brought someone with you.'

'Ah, yes, my dear—may I present Professor Baron van Tellerinck,' he added simply: 'His name's Raf.'

'Dutch,' said Mrs Bennett, and beamed at them both. 'On account of the "van", you know. I shall call you Raf.' She shook hands and rambled on: 'You sound very important—are you?'

'Not in the least, Mrs Bennett,' he ignored the other man's look, 'and I shall be delighted if you will call me Raf.'

Mrs Bennett tucked a hand into each of their arms. 'Come and meet a few people,' she invited. 'I've three daughters and they're all here. Ah, Ruth ... my youngest—she's just become engaged—so suitably too.'

Her daughter laughed and her mother added: 'This is Raf, dear, he's Dutch and says he's not important, but I don't believe him.'

Ruth shook hands. She was a pretty girl, on the small side, with brown curly hair and large hazel eyes. She said, 'Hullo, Raf, nice to meet you.' She put out a hand and caught hold of a girl on the point of passing them. 'Here's Jane.'

They were very alike: Jane had more vivid

colouring, perhaps, but they were the same height and size. The Dutchman shook hands and they stood talking for a few minutes until Mrs Bennett said that he must meet more of her friends. 'Katrina is around somewhere,' she told him vaguely. 'That's my eldest, of course.'

She plunged into a round of introductions, saw that he had a drink and presently left him. She was back within a few minutes with a tall, splendidly built girl beside her. 'Here she is; Katrina, this is Raf, he came with Uncle Ben.'

Katrina offered a cool hand and smiled politely, and then the smile turned into a cheerful grin as she saw the look of faint surprise on his face. 'I'm the odd one out,' she told him. 'Five feet ten inches and what's known as a large lady, no one ever believes that I'm one of the family. I take after my father, he was a big man and tall, almost as tall as you.'

She waited for him to speak and when he didn't felt disconcerted.

'Would you like another drink? I'll get . . .'

'Thank you, no.' His sleepy eyes were on her face, a pretty face with regular features and dark eyes, heavily fringed with long lashes. It made her feel even more disconcerted, so that she turned to the window and looked out, away from him. Outside the chilly March day was giving way to an even chillier evening; the pretty garden already glistening with a light drizzle. Katrina sighed and the Dutchman said: 'Your English spring is unpredictable, isn't it?'

She looked at him over her shoulder. 'Yes, I suppose that's why it's so delightful—though I prefer the autumn.'

His thick brows lifted and she went on, talking at random: 'Bonfires and apples and coming home to tea round the fire. Do you live in the country?'

'Oh yes, and I must agree about the bonfires and the apples; unfortunately we are not addicted as a nation to taking tea round the fire. I shall have to try it.'

She decided that he was difficult to talk to and sought feverishly for another topic of conversation and failed. 'I quite like the spring,' she observed idiotically.

His glance was grave, but she had the strongest suspicion that he was laughing at her. 'Ah, yes—"Oh, to be in England now that April's there". And a much nicer bit about May following . . .'

' "And after April, when May follows, and the whitethroat builds and all the swallows," ' Katrina quoted.

'You like Browning?'

'Well, yes, though I'm not all that keen on poetry.' She answered warily; if he was going to throw an Anthology of English Verse at her she was sunk. She said quickly: 'Do you have any Dutch poets?'

'Several, but none of them are much good at writing about the weather.'

She saw the smile at the corner of his firm mouth and thanked heaven silently as someone called her from across the room. 'Oh, there's someone . . . shall I introduce you to . . . ?'

She looked up into his face and saw his eyes twinkling. 'I'm very happy to remain here. I enjoyed our little talk about the weather—to be expected, of course—an English topic and so safe.'

Katrina felt her face pinken and was annoyed; he was laughing at her again and because he was a guest she couldn't tell him what she thought of him. She looked down her beautiful straight nose and said coldly: 'I hope you enjoy the rest of your visit to England, Professor,' and left him, feeling surprise at her feeling of regret that she would never see the tiresome man again. Just so that I could take him down a peg, she told herself as she joined a group of young people all talking at once. Their conversation seemed a little brash after the Professor's measured observations, but then of course he was much older; at least thirty-six or seven; she would find out from Uncle Ben.

It was later, when all the guests had gone and they were sitting round the fire drinking tea and eating the left-overs from the party for their supper, that Ruth observed: 'That was quite someone—the man Uncle Ben brought with him. If I weren't engaged to Edward I could go for him—he's a bit old, though.'

Katrina, to her surprise, found herself protesting. 'Not all that old, love. I daresay he's on the wrong side of thirty-five . . .'

'He's thirty-eight,' said her mother, 'I asked Ben. What were you talking about, Kate?'

'The weather.' Three pairs of blue eyes looked at her in surprise, and she frowned. 'Well,' she muttered, 'I'm so large—men don't chat up big women . . .'

'But you looked quite small beside him,' comforted her mother, 'and it must have been very nice for him not to have to bend double in order to talk to someone.' She looked puzzled. 'But the weather, darling?'

'I found him difficult to talk to.' Katrina yawned. 'Let's do the washing up and then I'm for bed; I must be off early in the morning.'

'When is your next holiday, dear?' Her mother piled cups and saucers and smiled across at her.

'Well, I can't be quite certain; Uncle Ben's got a backlog as long as my arm and as fast as there are a couple of beds empty they're filled by emergencies. I expect I'll wait until he's worked off most of his cases and decides to take a holiday himself.'

Katrina got to her feet and carried the tray down the stone-flagged passage to the kitchen where Amy, who had been with the family since she could remember, sat dozing by the Aga. She woke up as Katrina went in and said crossly: 'Now, Miss Kate, there's no call for you to be doing that.' She got out of her chair, a small round person with a sharp nose and small boot-button eyes.

Katrina put the tray down and gave Amy a hug. 'Go on with you!' she declared robustly. 'I've been standing around all the evening; a bit of washing up is just the exercise I need. Go to bed, Amy dear, do, and for heaven's sake call me in good time in the morning.'

Amy made only a token remonstrance. 'And you'll not go before you've had one of my breakfasts,' she declared. She sniffed. 'I daresay they starve you at that hospital.'

Katrina peered down at her splendidly proportioned person. 'Not so's it shows,' she observed.

She left soon after eight o'clock, driving herself in her rather battered Mini. The rain had ceased and it was a chilly morning with a pale sky holding a promise of spring. The house, standing back from the narrow street, looked delightful in the clear light, its grey stone walls softened by the ivy climbing them, its garden showing colour here and there where the daffodils were beginning to open; Katrina was reluctant to leave it and still more reluctant to leave her mother and sisters; they had always got on well, doubly so now that her father was dead. She waved to the various heads hanging from windows and turned into the street. There was no one much about; she passed the boys' school and turned into the main street through the town and presently joined the A30. London wasn't all that distance away and she had all the morning. She slowed through Shaftesbury and took the Salisbury road; she had done the trip so often that she knew just where she could push the little car to its limit and where it was better to slow down. She had time in hand by the time she reached Salisbury, and once through it, she stopped at Winterslow and had coffee, and not long after that she was on the M3, on the last leg of her journey.

Benedict's was an old hospital in name but very modern in appearance. The original building, empty now and awaiting demolition, lay on the north side of the river, strangled by narrow streets of ugly little houses, but now it was housed in a magnificent building, very impressive to look at, and fitted out with everything modern science could conceive of. It was a pity that there wasn't enough money left to staff it fully, especially as the nurses complained that it took them all their time to get from one part of the building to the other, for its corridors were end-less and staff weren't supposed to use the lifts.

Katrina, in charge of the men's surgical ward on the fourth floor, glanced up as she swept the Mini into the forecourt and housed it in the roomy garage to one side. It would be take-in week in the morning, she remembered. The ward had been full when she had left two days ago for her days off. Just for a moment she thought long-ingly of her home in the placid little Dorset town, which only bustled into life once a week on market day, but she had chosen to be a nurse and to train at a London teaching hospital, and she loved her work enough to stay in the city even though she disliked its rush and hurry.

She got her bag from the trunk and crossed to the side entrance, to climb to the second floor and cross by the covered bridge to the nurses' home. She had a bed-sitting room there in the airy cor-ridor set aside for the ward Sisters with its own door to shut them away from the student nurses, and a tiny kitchen as well as a generous supply of bathrooms, and above all, it held a nice sense of privacy. Katrina unlocked her door and went in. She had time enough to change, time to go to lunch if she wished, but she wasn't hungry; she set about the business of turning herself from a well-dressed young woman to a uniformed ward Sister, and while she did it, thought about the man Uncle Ben had brought with him to last night's party. She hadn't meant to think about him, and it annoyed her that somehow he had managed to pop into her head and wouldn't be dismissed. She forgot him presently, though, going back on duty a little early so that she could have a cup of tea before plunging into the rest of the day's work.

The ward was still full; true, two patients had gone home, but three had been admitted, which meant that there was already one bed in the middle of the ward and with take-in imminent, it would certainly be joined by several more.

Her senior staff nurse, Julie Friend, was on duty and Katrina breathed a sigh of relief; her second staff nurse, Moira Adams, was a tiresome creature, a self-important know-all, who bullied the nurses whenever she had the chance and irritated the patients, Katrina found her much more trying than all the patients put together and had told her so on various occasions, she had told the Senior Nursing Officer too, and that lady, although sympathetic, had pointed out that Adams would be leaving in a couple of months' time to take up a post in a surgical ward and she needed all the experience she could get. Katrina had thrust out her lower lip at that and wanted to know why the girl couldn't be transferred to the female block, only to be told that Adams would ride roughshod over Sister Jenkins. Which was true enough; Jilly Jenkins was a small sweet person and a splendid nurse, but she could be bullied . . .

Julie Friend was a different kettle of fish entirely. Katrina gave her a wide smile as she came in with the tea tray and put it on the desk, and

Julie returned it. She was a pretty girl, good at her job and popular, and saving hard to get married. Katrina, in her rare fits of depression, envied her wholeheartedly; Julie's Bill was a nice young man, a chemist in the hospital pharmacy and neither he nor Julie had any doubts about their future together, whereas Katrina had to admit to herself that she had any number of doubts about her own. She had had the opportunity enough to marry; she was a striking-looking girl and besides that, she had a little money of her own, a wide circle of the right kind of friends, and a comfortable home. She was quite a catch; it was a pity that those who had wanted to catch her were all small men. She hadn't had deep feelings about any of them, but she wondered from time to time if one of them had looked down at her instead of up, if she would have accepted him.

She poured their tea and listened to Julie's careful report, and after that, as Julie tactfully put it, there were one or two things . . .

They took half an hour to sort out: the laundry cutting up rough about extra sheets; the pharmacy being nasty about a prescription they couldn't read, the C.S.U. calling down doom upon her head because a pair of forceps were missing from one of the dressing packs, and one of the part-time nurses unable to come because of measles at home. Katrina dealt with them all in a calm manner and turned her attention to Julie's report again. Old Mr Crewe, who had been admitted as an emergency hernia four days ago and not quite himself after the operation, had been making both day and night hideous with his noisy demands for beer. Julie had reported that she had allowed him one with his lunch and been told, for her pains, that he had three or four pints at midday and the same again in the evening. Katrina chuckled and then frowned; she would have to think of something. She twitched her cap straight and got up to do a round.

It was one of the quietest times of the day; dinners were over and visitors wouldn't be coming just yet, the men were dozing or reading their papers or carrying on desultory conversations. Katrina went from bed to bed, stopping to chat with their occupants, filling in a pools coupon for a young man who had his right arm heavily bandaged, listening with patience and every appearance of interest while someone read her a long account of startling goings-on as reported in one of the more sensational newspapers; some of the patients were sleeping and two were still not quite round from anaesthetics. She checked their conditions carefully, gave soft-voiced instructions to one of the student nurses, and went on her way unhurriedly. She never appeared to hurry, and yet, as one nurse had observed to another, she was always there when she was needed.

Her round almost over, she tackled Mr Crewe, eyeing her belligerently from his bed. 'And what's all this about beer?' she asked composedly.

She let the old man have his say and then said reasonably: 'Well, you know if you have eight or nine pints of beer each day, we simply can't afford to keep you here. Have you anyone at home to look after you?'

'Me wife.'

'Anyone else?'

'I've got a daughter lives close by. Sensible she is, not like the old girl.'

Katrina thought for a bit. 'Look, let's make a bargain; you can have a pint at dinner time and another with your supper and I'll see if we can get you home a couple of days earlier. Mind you, you'll have to behave yourself.'

His promise was of the piecrust variety, she knew that, but at least it meant temporary peace.

A peace they needed during the next few days; it seemed as though everyone in the vicinity of the hospital was bent on falling off ladders, tripping over pavements or being nudged by buses. Usually there were broken bones involved, but for some reason this week it was cuts and bruises and concussion, so that none of the victims went to the orthopaedic block but arrived with monotonous regularity in the surgical ward.

It was on the last day on take-in, with the cheering prospect of Mr Crewe going home very shortly and a hard week's work behind them all, when things began to go wrong. Julie went off sick for a start, which meant that Katrina wouldn't be able to have her days off and Moira Adams, taking advantage of Julie's absence and Katrina's preoccupation with her patients, began chivvying the junior nurses. Katrina, coming upon a tearful girl behind the sluice door, had to take Moira into her office and rake her down, pointing out as she did so that she was having to waste time which could have been spent to much greater advantage on the patients. Moira pouted

and argued until Katrina said sharply, 'That's
enough, Staff, you should know better, and you'll
never get anyone to work for you if you bully
them.' She glanced at her watch and saw with
relief that it was after five o'clock and Moira was
due off duty—better still, she had days off as
well. Katrina felt relief flood through her, but
none of it showed; she said with quiet authority:
'Go off duty, Staff.'

It was lucky that she had two second-year student nurses on duty, both good hard-working
girls, as well as the tearful little creature who was
still apparently in the sluice. Katrina swept
through the ward, her eyes everywhere; nothing
seemed amiss. She reached the sluice and found
Nurse James, washing a red, puffy face under the
cold water tap. 'The thing is,' began Katrina
without preamble, 'you have to learn not to mind,
Nurse James. There'll always be someone you
can't see eye to eye with, someone who'll try and
upset you. Well, don't let them—you're a very
junior nurse at present, but if you work hard
you'll be a good one one day and these upsets will
have been worth while. Now come into the ward
with me; we're going to do the medicine round
together.'

The evening went swiftly after that, there was
so much to do: cases from the morning's list
needing to be settled; dressed in their own pyja-
mas again, given drinks, gently washed and when
they could be, sat up. The four of them had to
work hard but by first supper, Katrina was able
to send the two senior girls to their meal; there
was only one case which bothered her and she

had already sent a message to the registrar to come and see the man the moment that he was free. The man had been admitted that morning after an accident in which he had had an arm crushed so badly that it had been amputated. He had come round nicely from the anaesthetic and the surgeon had seen him and pronounced himself satisfied, and although Katrina could see nothing wrong she thought that the man looked far more poorly than he should. It was no joke, losing an arm, but he was a powerfully built young man and healthy. They had settled him nicely against his pillows and he had had a cup of tea and the drip was running well. All the same she was uneasy. Leaving Nurse James to trot round the ward, making sure that the men were comfortable, she went along to write the report in her office, only to go back again to the man's bedside on the pretext of checking his chart. He looked worse, so much so that she drew the curtains around the bed and bent over him with a cheerful: 'Sorry to disturb you, I just want to make sure that your dressing's nice and firm, still.'

The dressing was all right, but there was an ominous red stain seeping through the bandage. There was a tray on the locker by the bed with everything needed for just such a happening. Katrina put on a pad and bandage, binding it firmly and pretended to adjust the drip while she watched. Something was very wrong; already the blood was oozing through the package she had only just put on.

'How do you feel?' she asked the man. 'There's

a little bleeding and you may feel a bit faint, but it's nothing to worry about.' She smiled reassuringly at him and called softly: 'Nurse James!'

She was busy re-packing yet again when she heard the girl behind her. 'Go to the office, please, Nurse,' she said in her usual unhurried manner, 'and tell the porter to get Mr Reynolds at once. He must come here immediately. Tell them it's urgent. If he's not available then any house surgeon will do. Be quick and come back as fast as you can.' She hadn't turned round, she heard Nurse James say: 'Yes, Sister,' and added: 'Is the ward O.K.?'

'Quite O.K.,' said Uncle Ben from behind her. 'In trouble, Sister?'

She was applying pressure now and didn't look up. Dear Uncle Ben, arriving just when she needed him most. 'An amputation this morning; he recovered well, but his blood pressure has been dropping very slowly. Mr Reynolds came to see him this afternoon and found everything satisfactory. This has just started—five-six minutes ago.'

Uncle Ben gave a little cough. 'Well, we'd better have a quick look—got some forceps handy?'

She turned back the towel covering the tray and was on the point of taking up the scissors when a large hand took them from her.

'That's right, Raf—let's get this off and see the damage. Sister, send your nurse to theatre and tell them I want it ready in five minutes. I shall want four litres of blood too—get on to the Path Lab., will you?'

Nurse James had come back with the news that there was a major accident just in and there was no one available right away. 'Never mind, Nurse—Sir Benjamin is here, so we're all right. Now go to theatre, will you . . .' She passed on Uncle Ben's wishes and turned back to the patient. He was semi-conscious by now and the bandages and dressing were off. 'Dear, dear,' observed Uncle Ben in his mildest voice. 'Apply pressure, Sister, will you? Raf, can you get at it with the forceps while I swab?'

Professor van Tellerinck, in waistcoat and shirt sleeves, somehow contrived to look elegant despite the messy job he was doing. He was very efficient too; Katrina's head was almost fully occupied with what she was doing, but a tiny corner of it registered that fact, and another one too, that she was pleased to see him again, which seemed strange since she hadn't liked him over-much. Probably it was just relief at his timely help. He hadn't spoken to her, indeed, she wasn't sure that he had even looked at her; in the circumstances that was to be expected. He had found the slipped ligature and had put on a Spencer Wells and the two men were carefully checking that there was no further trouble.

Uncle Ben unbent slowly. 'Something big in the Accident Room, did I hear Nurse say? In that case, Raf, be good enough to give me a hand, will you?'

The theatre trolley and the two student nurses arrived together. Katrina told one of them to go with the patient to theatre and with the help of the other nurse, started to clear up; it took some time to get everything clean and ready for the man's return and it was time for the nurses to go off duty when they had done. Katrina sent them away and greeted the night nurses with the suggestion that they should get started with their evening routine while she got down to the report. She had written it, read it to the night staff nurse and was back in her office when the patient came back, and because the two nurses were changing a dressing and there was no one else available, she saw him safely back into his bed, still groggy from the anaesthetic. She was checking the drip when Uncle Ben arrived and wanted to know why she was still there and when she explained, he gave a snort of impatience and walked off to the Office to telephone.

Katrina hadn't realised that the Professor was there too, standing quietly watching her. His silence was a little unnerving, and, as she knew that despite the fact that she had cleaned herself up as best she could she looked a mess, her pretty features assumed a haughtiness which sat ill upon them.

'I wouldn't have believed it,' observed the Professor suddenly. 'When we met I assumed you to be a young lady of leisure with nothing more on her mind than the latest fashions and the current boy-friend.'

She gave him a cross look and said peevishly: 'Indeed? Just as I was amazed to find that you were a surgeon.'

He looked amused. 'Oh, should I look like one?'

She ignored that. 'I had the strong impression

that you did nothing at all.'

'Oh, dear—we seem to have started off on the
wrong foot, don't we?'

Several rather pert answers flashed through her
tired mind. Luckily she had no opportunity of
uttering any of them, for Mr Crewe, his supper
pint already forgotten, was demanding more beer.
'Excuse me,' said Katrina austerely, and went
into the ward to do battle, telling the junior night
nurse to stay with the man until he was quite
round from his anaesthetic. She subdued Mr
Crewe quietly but briskly, did a quick round to
wish her patients goodnight and went back to the
Office, where she tidied her desk and thought
about the Professor. She had to admit that she
had been surprised to discover that he was a surgeon, he had given all the appearance of the man
of leisure and she had gained the impression,
quite erroneously, as it had turned out, that he
was—well, lazy, at least easygoing, but he had
done a very neat job without fuss. And so he
ought, if he's anything of a surgeon, she muttered
to herself as she swept the last lot of papers into a
drawer, yawning widely as she did so; it had been
a long day.

And not over yet, it seemed. Uncle Ben,
coming in as she was on the point of going out,
stopped her with a brisk: 'Finished, Kate? You'll
have had no supper, I'll be bound—I'll take you
back with me for a meal. Go and clean yourself
up and be downstairs in ten minutes.'

Professor van Tellerinck had followed her
uncle. He was leaning against the wall now, smiling a little, which needled her so much that she

said far too quickly. 'That's awfully kind of you, Uncle Ben, but I can get something on my way to the home. It's far too late to bother Aunt Lucy. Will the man do?'

'I think so. We found another slipped ligature, but he's well and truly tied now. By the way, I asked Night Sister to send someone along to keep an eye on him for a few hours. Now hurry up, girl, or your aunt will nag me.'

Katrina chuckled. Aunt Lucy was a dear little dumpling of a woman who had never nagged anyone in her life; she had the kindest of hearts and a sunny disposition and spoilt Uncle Ben quite shamelessly.

'All right, I'd love to come if I won't be a nuisance.'

She parted with the two men at the ward doors, sternly recommended by Uncle Ben not to be more than the time he had stated, and not quite sure whether she should say goodbye to his companion or not. She compromised with a social smile and a little nod.

She showered and changed into a silk blouse and a pleated skirt and topped them with a thick knitted jacket. With her hair unpinned from the rather severe style she wore under her cap, and hanging about her shoulders, she looked prettier than ever, but she wasted little time on either her face or her hair. With barely a minute to spare she raced through the hospital to the front entrance, to find Uncle Ben there and the Dutchman as well. She wasn't sure if she was pleased or annoyed about that, but she was given no time to decide. Uncle Ben caught her by the arm and hurried her across the courtyard to fetch up beside a Bentley Corniche.

Katrina, breathing rather rapidly because she had had to hurry, and looking quite magnificent, let out a loud sigh.

'Uncle Ben, is it yours? It's super!'

'Don't be a fool, my dear, it's Raf's.'

She glanced at the Dutchman and found him watching her, his sleepy eyes alert beneath their lids. She said rather lamely: 'Oh, how nice,' and watched his smile as he opened the door and ushered her into the front seat. Probably he drove abominably, she told herself as Uncle Ben made himself comfortable in the back and the Professor got behind the wheel. But he didn't, he drove superbly, placidly unconcerned with the traffic around them, taking advantage of every foot of space, using the big car's power to slide past everything else. Katrina allowed herself to relax thankfully and just for a moment closed her eyes.

'Never tell me you're tired,' murmured the Professor in a hatefully soft voice, 'a great strapping girl like you.'

'I am not . . .' began Katrina in a strangled voice, and stopped; he was trying to make her lose her temper, and she wasn't going to. 'You're not exactly a lightweight yourself,' she observed sweetly.

'For which I am profoundly thankful,' he assured her. 'I like to look down on my women.'

'I am not,' said Katrina in a furious rush, 'one of your women!'

'Oh, no, you don't resemble any of the girls I know—they're slim and small and mostly plaintive.'

'I'm not surprised,' she snapped, 'if they know you.'

He had a nice laugh. 'I think we're going to enjoy getting to know each other, Kate.'

They were in Highgate Village now, close to Uncle Ben's house, and as he slowed and stopped before its gate she had what she hoped was the last word. 'Think what you like, Professor van Tellerinck, but I have no wish to get to know you.'

He only laughed again.

CHAPTER TWO

UNCLE Ben's house was a Regency villa standing in its own immaculately kept garden, well back from the road. Aunt Lucy flung the door wide as they got out of the car and began to speak almost before they had got within earshot.

'Katrina, how lovely—your supper's waiting for you. Ben dear, how fortunate that it was something I was able to keep hot. Raf, you must be famished!'

She bustled them through the hall and into the sitting-room, furnished with easy chairs and sofas and a number of small tables, loaded down with knitting, books and newspapers. 'Mary's just dishing up—you'll have time for a drink.'

Katrina had her coat whisked from her and was sat in a chair and a drink put into her hand. 'Ben said on the phone that you've had a busy evening,' went on Aunt Lucy, happily unaware of what the business entailed. 'I was a bit put out when the men were called away just as we were about to sit down to table, but this makes up for it. How is your dear mother?'

The men had taken their drinks to the wide french window at the end of the room after responding suitably to Aunt Lucy's greeting, and now she cast them an indulgent glance. 'I suppose they'll mull over whatever it was for the rest of the evening, which means that we can have a nice gossip.'

Aunt Lucy's voice was soothing and the sherry gave Katrina an uplift she badly needed, and by some domestic magic conjured up by the cook, the meal which they sat down to presently was delicious. Katrina, thoroughly famished, fell to with a good appetite, avoiding the Professor's eye and only addressing him directly when he spoke to her.

Which wasn't often, and then with a casual politeness which she found annoying, despite the fact that she had decided that she really didn't like him at all. She was taken completely off guard presently, when, dinner over and coffee drunk in the sitting room, she murmured to her aunt that she would have to go. The two men were standing together, discussing some case or other, but the Professor interrupted what he was saying to observe;

'I'll run you back, Katrina.'

'There's no need, thank you—I'll get a taxi.'

'I have to go back anyway to pick up some instruments.' He spoke blandly, ignoring her reply, and Aunt Lucy at once backed him up.

'Well, of course, if you're really going that way—so much nicer than a taxi at this time of night, Kate—someone to talk to, as well,' she added happily.

Katrina thought of that remark ten minutes later, sitting beside the Professor in the Bentley, trying hard to think of some topic of conversation. She scowled horribly when he observed placidly: 'Considering that it will be April in a few days' time, the evenings are surprisingly chilly.'

'Why are you in England?' asked Katrina, not bothering with the weather.

'Interested? I'm flattered. Your uncle and I are old friends—he knew my father well. When I come to England I like to see him.'

Which hadn't answered her question. 'You're a surgeon, too?'

'Yes.' He turned the car into the hospital yard and parked it. 'No, stay there,' he told her, and got out and opened the door for her. 'Such a pleasant evening,' he murmured. 'Goodnight, Kate.'

She suspected that he was amused about something again. Her goodnight was civil but nothing more. Going slowly up the stairs of the nurses' home to her room, she reflected that she wouldn't see him again and was surprised at her glum feelings about that. She had hoped, with conventional politeness, that he would enjoy the rest of his stay in England, and all he had said was that he was quite sure that he would.

'Oh, well,' she said crossly as she opened her door, 'who cares? I shan't be seeing him again, anyway.'

She saw him the very next afternoon. It had been a simply beastly morning, with Mr Knowles doing a round of his six beds and spinning it out to a quite unnecessary length of time, so that dinners were late, nurses didn't get off duty on time, and Katrina herself had had to be content with cheese sandwiches and a pot of tea in the office. And if that wasn't enough, she had been waylaid by Jack Bentall, one of the house surgeons, and badgered into a reluctant promise to go out to

dinner with him in a couple of days' time. Despite the fact that she had never encouraged him,
he waylaid her on every possible occasion, making
no secret of his feelings, even allowing it to be
bruited around that she was quite bowled over by
him. Katrina had never lacked for invitations; she
was a delightful companion and sufficiently lovely
for men to like to be seen out with her, but she had
never taken any of them seriously. For one thing,
as she had pointed out so many times to her
mother and sisters, she was so large . . .

But Jack Bentall didn't seem to mind that; he
was a rather short, thickset young man, and con-
ceited, and nothing Katrina could say would con-
vince him that she didn't care two straws for him.
Usually she fobbed him off, but today she had
been tired and put out and had lost some of her
fire, and even though she regretted it bitterly
already, she was far too honest to invent an
excuse at the last minute. But it would be the last
time, she promised herself, as she gobbled up the
sandwiches and went back to the ward.

The nurses were tidying beds before the visitors were admitted and had prudently left Mr
Crewe until the last. They had just reached him
as Katrina opened the doors and her ears were
assailed at once by his voice raised in anger. 'A
pint ain't enough,' he bellowed. 'I wants me
usual—'alf an alf an' a couple more ter settle the
first pint.'

'You'll be lucky,' observed Katrina,' and I
thought you wanted to go home? Here you are
lying in bed—if you're not well enough to sit out
in your chair, Mr Crewe, then you're not well

enough to have a pint of beer. You promised me . . .'

'Pah,' said Mr Crewe grumpily, 'I want ter go 'ome.'

'Yes, I know that, Mr Crewe, and I promised you that you should go a day or two earlier if you kept your side of the bargain—which you're not.'

Mr Crewe opened his mouth to say, 'Pah,' again and changed it to, 'Oo's that—I see'd 'im yesterday . . .'

He was staring down the ward, for the moment forgetful of his beer. 'Big chap,' he added, and Katrina's head, before she could stop it, shot round to take a look. Professor Baron van Tellerinck, no less, coming round to take a look down the ward with unhurried calm. He wished her good afternoon gravely, and just as gravely greeted Mr Crewe, who said rudely: ''ullo—'oo are you?'

'A colleague of Sir Benjamin,' the Professor told him equably, 'and as I have business with Sister I'm sure you will do as you are asked and sit in your chair and—er—keep quiet.'

And much to Katrina's astonishment, Mr Crewe meekly threw back the bedclothes and got into the dressing gown one of the nurses was holding.

'You wished to see a patient?' asked Katrina, at her most professional.

'Please. Sir Benjamin can't get away from theatre at present, he asked me if I would check up on Mr Miles.'

She liked him for that; so many surgeons came on to the ward and asked: 'Sister, I'd like to see that gastric ulcer you admitted,' or: 'How is that lacerated hand doing?' for all the world as if the ward beds were occupied by various portions of anatomy and not people.

'He's coming along nicely,' she observed, quite forgetting to be stiff. 'His B.P.'s down and he's eating well. We've had him out of bed for a little while this morning.'

The Professor spent five minutes or so with the patient, expressed himself satisfied with his progress, wished him a polite good day, and started up the ward towards the office. 'If I might just write up the notes?' he enquired, and when she opened the door and then turned to go: 'Please stay, Sister.'

So she stayed, waiting silently while he scrawled on the chart, added his initials and then got to his feet. 'Doing anything this evening?' he asked her.

'Me?' she was so surprised that she had no words for a moment. 'I'm off at five o'clock,' she added stupidly.

'Yes, I know that,' and when her eyes looked a question, 'I looked in the off duty book on my way in,' he explained blandly, and waited for her to answer.

'Well . . .' she paused. 'It's very kind of you, but I'm not sure . . .'

He interrupted her: 'That's why it would be a good idea if we got to know each other,' he observed placidly. A remark which left her totally bewildered, and before she could answer: 'There's a rather nice place in Ebury Street we might go to—a bistro, perhaps you know of it?'

She shook her head, still trying to think of

something to say.

'La Poule au Pot, although you might prefer to go somewhere else?'

She found herself saying just as meekly as Mr Crewe had acted: 'It sounds very nice. Is it a dressy place?'

He smiled, 'No, I think not,' and watched her, still smiling while one corner of her brain was turning over her wardrobe for a suitable dress. 'I'm sure you're thinking that you'll have nothing to wear, women always do, don't they? I'm equally sure that you have. Shall we say seven o'clock at the entrance.'

He smiled again as he left the office, leaving Katrina to wonder if she had actually said that she would go out with him. She didn't think that she had, but it was a little too late for that now.

She got off duty late; it had been that sort of a day, and her nerves were jangling with a desire to allow her ill humour to have full rein, instead of having to present a calm good-tempered face to patients and nurses alike. But a leisurely bath did her a power of good, by the time she had found a dress to her liking—a sapphire blue silk jersey, very simply cut—done her hair in a low roll round her head in an Edwardian hair-style, and got into a pair of high-heeled black patent shoes, she felt quite herself again. She picked up a velvet jacket and took a last look at herself in the mirror. For some reason she wanted to look nice this evening; she had told herself that it was because she didn't like the Professor, which to her at least made sense in a roundabout way, and at least, she told herself as she started downstairs, she could wear high-heeled shoes without being in danger of towering over her escort.

She was ten minutes late, but he was waiting for her with no sign of impatience, only smiled gently as he glanced at her from hooded eyes.

'Ah, the wardrobe wasn't quite empty, I see.'

Katrina found herself smiling too and uttered her thought out loud without thinking. 'You have no idea how nice it is to go out with someone who's taller than I—even in low heels I loom over most people.'

He glanced down at her elegant feet on their three-inch heels. 'I have the same difficulty, only in reverse; I find it so tiresome to bend double each time I want to mutter sweet nothings into my companion's ear.'

'Well, you won't need to worry about that,' declared Katrina sharply.

'Oh, I wasn't,' he told her silkily as he opened the car door. 'I need only bend my head to you, Kate.'

She peeped at him to see if he was laughing, but he looked quite serious and she frowned; it was a remark which she found difficult to answer, so she said nothing, but got into the car, to be instantly lulled by its comfort as they edged into the evening traffic, and her feeling of pleasure increased as they went along; it was decidedly pleasant to be driven in a shining black Bentley towards a good meal. Moreover, the Professor was laying himself out to be pleasant, talking about nothing much in an amusing manner; she almost liked him.

She wondered later, as she got ready for bed,

what exactly she had expected of their evening, but whatever it was, it hadn't happened. Her host had been charming in a coolly friendly way and they had talked ... She stopped to remember what they had talked about—everything under the sun, and yet she knew nothing about him, for he had taken care not to tell her anything and when she had asked from which part of Holland he came, he had said merely that his family came from the north—Friesland, but he lived within striking distance of Leiden. Whether he was married or no, she had no idea, and although it had been on the tip of her tongue to ask just that, she had stopped herself just in time. She had, she reflected as she brushed her hair, absolutely no reason for wishing to know.

The restaurant had been charming, cosy and warm, with blazing fires at either end of the quite small room and soft candlelight to eat their dinner by. And the food had been delicious; smoked salmon, *noisettes d'agneau Beauharnais* with artichoke hearts and *pommes de terre Berny*, followed by a purée of sweet chestnuts with whipped cream. Katrina smacked her lips at the thought of them and jumped into bed. They had sat over their meal and it was past midnight now, but the evening had flown and when she had said goodbye to him at the hospital entrance, she had felt regret that it couldn't last longer. Perhaps, she mused sleepily, she rather liked him after all. 'Such a pity,' she muttered, 'because I'll never know now; he didn't say he wanted to see me again. I expect he was being polite because he knows Uncle Ben.'

If the Professor was being polite then he was carrying it to excess. He accompanied Uncle Ben on his round the next day and when Katrina escorted them to the ward door and took a formal leavetaking of them, he asked her, with Uncle Ben looking on, if she would care to go to the theatre with him that evening.

Katrina's mouth was forming 'No,' even as her heart sang 'Yes,' but she had no chance to utter, for Uncle Ben said at once: 'What a splendid idea—just what you need, Kate, after a hard day's grind.' He asked the Professor: 'What's on?'

'I've got tickets for *The King and I*.' The hooded eyes were on Katrina's face. 'That is, if Kate would like to see it?'

A show she had wanted to see more than anything else, but how could he possibly know that?

'Going all tarted up?' enquired Uncle Ben with interest.

'Er—I thought we might have supper and perhaps dance afterwards.'

My almost new organza, thought Katrina wildly, and those satin sandals. Aloud she said: 'Well, I don't know ...'

'Rubbish,' said Uncle Ben stoutly. 'You know you like dancing, Kate.'

The two of them stared at her without saying anything more, so that in sheer self-defence she said: 'Well, it would be nice ... thank you.'

'Half past seven at the entrance,' said the Professor briskly. 'We'll just have time for a drink and a bite to eat before the theatre.'

She asked meekly: 'And am I to come all tarted up?'

'Oh, definitely—that's if you feel like it . . .' He was laughing at her again, although his face was bland.

'Well, that's settled, then,' declared Uncle Ben. 'Raf, there's that woman I want you to see—the accident that came in during the night . . .'

Katrina excused herself and left them deep in some surgical problem. She had problems of her own; it was so much simpler to either like or dislike someone, but with the Professor she was unable to make up her mind. Most of the time, she had to admit, she liked him very much, but every now and then he annoyed her excessively. She went back into the ward and found to her annoyance that Jack Bentall had come in through the balcony doors and was doing a round with Julie. He had, he explained carefully, one or two things to write up for Mr Knowles and could he use her office for a few minutes, and as Julie left them: 'You haven't forgotten that we're going out tomorrow evening?' he asked her, looking quite revoltingly smug. She had, but she was too kindhearted to say so.

He was disposed to linger, hinting at the delights of their evening out so that she had to draw his attention to several jobs awaiting her. He had looked at her like a small spoilt boy and said grumpily: 'Oh, well, don't let me keep you . . .'

She wished with all her heart that she had refused his invitation in the first place. She had been a fool, but there was no help for it, she would go, but for the last time, she promised herself, and then forgot all about him, going from one patient to the next, adjusting drips, checking dressings, making sure that B.P.s had been taken on time.

She was a little absentminded at dinner time and her friends wanted to know why, and when she shook her head and denied it, Joan Cox from Women's Surgical said vigorously: 'I bet our Kate's got herself a date with that super man who's doing the rounds with Sir Benjamin,' and the entire table gave a howl of laughter when Katrina went a delicate pink.

'Didn't I say so?' cried Joan triumphantly, and then thoughtfully: 'You went out yesterday evening too.'

'Well, yes, I did—just to a bistro . . .'

'And is it to be a bistro tonight?' several voices chorused.

'*The King and I*.' Katrina poured tea from the large pot just put on the table.

'And dinner afterwards, I expect, and a spot of dancing?'

'Well, the Professor did say something about it . . .'

There was another howl of laughter. 'Kate, you don't call him Professor, do you? What's his name—what do you talk about?'

'The weather,' said Katrina guilelessly.

The afternoon went quickly. She handed over to Julie at five o'clock, did a final round to wish the patients goodnight, and went off duty. She had plenty of time, time to lie for ages in the bath, make up her lovely face at her leisure and wind her hair into its intricate chignon before putting on the organza dress. It was a lovely thing, patterned in shades of amber and brown

with a square yoke and a waist tied by long satin
ribbons, its balloon sleeves ending in tight bands
at her elbows. Her slippers were exactly right
with it, as was the brown marabou stole she dug
out from the back of the wardrobe.

He had said half past seven, and she took care
to be on time this evening, even though she was
held up for a few minutes by some of her friends
who had come to inspect her outfit. Their cheerful teasing voices followed her down the stairs
and then were abruptly shut off by the nurses'
home door. It was quiet as she went through the
hospital corridors: it was visiting time again and
nurses would be at first supper while the rest
finished the tidying up for the day. The sudden
lack of voices worried her. Supposing he wasn't
there? Supposing she had made a mistake in the
evening—supposing he hadn't meant it? All silly
ideas, but all the same they loomed large. Just
until she came in sight of the entrance, to see him
standing there, enormous, reassuringly calm and
very elegant indeed.

His hullo was friendly, as was his: 'How
charming you look, Katrina, and punctual too.'

She wondered fleetingly if he said that to all
the girls he took out, for undoubtedly there must
be girls ... She said, 'Thank you,' in a guarded
tone, and he laughed and said ruefully: 'It doesn't
matter what I say, does it? You see a hidden
meaning in every word I utter.'

They were walking to the car, but now she
stopped. 'Look, we can't possibly start the evening like this—I—didn't mean ... that is, I was
only wondering if you said that to all the girls you

take out.'

'Would you mind if I said yes?'

She said haughtily: 'Of course not,' and spoilt it by asking: 'Do you go out a great deal?'

They were in the car now, but he hadn't started the engine. 'Yes, quite a bit, but work comes first. What about you, Katrina?'

'Well, I go out—I like my work too,' she added with a bit of a rush.

'We share a common interest, then.' He started the car. 'We have time for a drink if you would like one.'

He took her to the Savoy and gave her a glass of Madeira, and when she confessed that she had had no tea, a dish of salted nuts and another of potato crisps.

She crunched her way very nearly through the lot and then said apologetically: 'I'm making a pig of myself. It was stew for lunch and I got there late.'

His winged nostrils flared. 'Tepid and greasy, no doubt.' He lifted a finger and when the waiter came, asked for sandwiches. She consumed them with the unselfconscious pleasure of a child— smoked salmon and pâté de foie gras and cucumber. But she refused a second glass of Madeira because, as she explained to her companion, she wanted to enjoy every moment of the play.

Which she did, sitting up straight in her seat, her eyes glued to the stage, and the Professor, sitting a little sideways so that he could watch her as well as the stage, allowed himself a faint smile at her obvious pleasure. They went back to the Savoy when it was over and had supper—caviar,

poularde Impératrice, and for Katrina a bûche gla-
cée, while the Professor contented himself with
Welsh rarebit. And because, as he had gravely
pointed out to her at the beginning of the meal,
they had both had a tiring day, a bottle of champagne seemed the best thing to drink.

Katrina, her head still full of romantic music,
would have happily drunk tap water; as it was,
she drank two glasses of champagne and enjoyed
them very much. There was a faint worry at the
back of her head that she was liking her companion much more than she had intended. Perhaps it was the combination of romance and
champagne which had dimmed her good sense,
but certainly he seemed really rather nice. When
he suggested that they might dance she got up at
once. She might be a big girl, but she danced well
and was as light as a feather, and the Professor
was pretty neat on his feet too. They danced for a
long time, going back to drink their coffee and
then taking to the floor again. It was past one
o'clock when Katrina asked him the time, and
gave a small screech when he told her.

'I'm on in the morning, and it's Mr Knowles'
round and take-in.'

He didn't try to persuade her to stay but drove
her back to the hospital without fuss and saw her
to the door, and when she thanked him for her
lovely evening, observed placidly that he had enjoyed it too, then he wished her goodnight and
opened the door for her.

Katrina went through feeling let down; not so
much as a hint that he wanted to see her again, let
alone the kiss which she had come to expect at

the close of an evening out. The horrid thought that he had asked her out because Uncle Ben had suggested it crossed her mind; Uncle Ben knew how shy she was about going out with men who weren't her size, and here was one who positively towered over her. He hadn't said goodbye, she mused as she tumbled into bed; a clever girl would have known how to find out when and where he was going ... and anyway, she asked herself pettishly, why was she worried? She didn't like him, did she? Or did she? She was too sleepy to decide.

The morning began badly with two road accidents being admitted just after eight o'clock, and it got worse as the day wore on, so that when Jack Bentall rather fussily examined Mr Knowles' patients during the afternoon, demanding unnecessary attention and calling for things he didn't really need, she found her patience wearing thin. The urge to cry off the evening's entertainment was very strong, but she was a kindhearted girl and she had refused to go out with him on so many occasions she couldn't avoid this one without hurting his feelings. Not that she minded about that over-much; he was a young man of unbounded conceit and she doubted if even the severest snub would affect him for more than a few minutes.

She dressed unwillingly and went just as unwillingly to the car park where Jack had asked her to meet him. He drove a souped-up Mini, very battered and uncomfortable and he tended to regard the road as his. She felt a pang of relief as he stopped with a teeth-jarring suddenness in front of a Chinese restaurant in the Tottenham Court Road. It was unfortunate that Katrina didn't like Chinese food and that Jack hadn't thought to ask her. Now if it had been the Professor, with all his faults, she added mentally, he would have made it his business to find out. And even if he hadn't, she mused with surprise, she would have felt quite at liberty to have told him that she loathed sweet and sour pork and could have asked him if they could go somewhere else. But Jack would either laugh at her and tell her that she didn't know good food when she saw it, or worse, sulk.

She ate her way through a great many dishes without once betraying her dislike of them, listening to Jack, carrying on about the other housemen and their inefficiencies, what Mr Knowles had said to him and he had said to Mr Knowles; he droned on and on and Katrina's thoughts turned more and more to the previous evening. Professor van Tellerinck might annoy her, although she wasn't sure why any more—but he didn't bore her. She came out of a flurry of half-formed thoughts to hear Jack say:

'Well, what about it? Everyone else does it these days and getting married seems a bit silly until I've reached the top, and you're not all that keen on it, are you? You can't be—you must have had plenty of chances, but after all, you are twenty-seven.'

She gave him a look of such astonishment that he added querulously: 'Well, you don't have to look like that—I thought we understood each other.'

As well as being astonished she was furiously angry, but she discovered at the same time that she simply couldn't be bothered to explain to him just how wrong he was. She could of course have said: 'I am a clergyman's daughter and old-fashioned in my views about matrimony'; instead she heard herself saying in a reasonable voice: 'I really should have told you sooner, Jack, but I didn't realise...' She left the sentence hanging delicately in mid-air. 'I've resigned—I'm going abroad in a few weeks' time.' She paused, trying to think of a country as far away as possible: 'The Gulf—a lovely job.' Her imagination was working well by now. 'One of those new hospitals, a fabulous salary and a flat of my own...'

He looked at her gobbling with rage. 'Well, you could have told me before we came out to dinner!' he said furiously. He put a hand up for the bill. 'I don't suppose you want coffee.'

They tore back to Benedict's through the almost empty streets and as he came to a squealing halt in the forecourt: 'I hope you get what you deserve!' he hissed at her.

Just as though I'd led him on, thought Katrina as she went into the nurses' home, and giggled. She stopped giggling almost at once, though. She would have to resign in the morning; she had done herself out of a job and banished herself to the Gulf to boot. Jack would tell everyone, he was a noted gossip, and really there was nothing she could do about it but leave; even if she explained to him why she had done it, he wouldn't understand but would merely think that she had been playing hard to get and would pester her more than ever. She lay awake for a long time getting more and more worried, and fell asleep at last with her mind in a dither.

CHAPTER THREE

SHE was still dithering when she got reluctantly out of bed a few hours later, but by the time she had dressed she knew for a certainty that she would go to the office directly after breakfast and tender her resignation to Miss Bowles. She stopped doing her hair and sat down on the edge of the bed to write out her resignation, then finished dressing in a rush so as to be in time for breakfast. As it was, she was late, which was a blessing for no one had time to ask her any questions.

Miss Bowles asked questions, though. She was a small peppery lady well into her fifties, who ruled the hospital with a rod of iron whatever the National Health Service said. There wasn't much that she approved of, and certainly not Katrina going off to the Gulf. She demanded all the details of the mythical post, too, and Katrina was forced to say firmly that she was still waiting for all the details.

'Well, Sister,' said Miss Bowles, in an ill humour now because one of the best ward Sisters was leaving, 'I hope you know what you're about. You have a good post here and prospects of promotion in the future. I only hope you're not throwing security away for some pipe dream in the desert.'

Katrina longed to tell her that it was a pipe

dream, but the repercussions if she did weren't to
be contemplated. She would go home for a holiday and then set about getting another job, well
away from London. Abroad, perhaps? There was
surely no reason why she should think of Holland?

She didn't tell any of her friends straight away;
for one thing, she had no opportunity, it was that
evening when she went off duty that she told
them as they sat around in their sitting-room,
mulling over the day among themselves.

'But you can't!' they chorused. 'Kate, why?
There must be some reason . . .'

'I need a change,' she told them, 'I'm going to
have a holiday at home and then go abroad. The
Gulf,' she added vaguely, mindful of the hospital
grapevine and Jack, not to mention Miss Bowles,
who in her own dignified manner would allow the
news to seep through the upper strata of admin.
staff.

She had a few days' holiday due to her, which
meant that she could leave in just about three
weeks' time. She would go home on her next days
off and explain to her mother, and until then she
would go on with her work in a normal manner.
Easier said than done; she worried a good deal
about her future, trying to make up her mind just
where she wanted to go and she still had to tell
Uncle Ben, not a real uncle at all, but he had been
her father's closest friend and had kept an eye on
them ever since her father's death.

But not just yet, it seemed. Uncle Ben had a
severe cold and couldn't operate or do his rounds;
his registrar coped in his absence until a nasty

traffic accident, full of complications, made it needful for him to call in a consultant.

Katrina supposed she wasn't surprised to see Professor van Tellerinck with the registrar at his heels, come down the ward. She had imagined him back home in his own country, but she had no means of knowing where he was; probably he'd been close at hand all the time. She greeted him civilly, led him to the patient and waited quietly while he went over the man's severe injuries. The leg could be saved, he thought, given a few hours' repair work in theatre, but he wasn't sure about the arm. He arranged for the man to go to theatre that afternoon, and made his way to the door, the registrar beside him, Katrina, one pace behind, ready to bid him good-day at the ward door.

But once there, he paused, suggested in the nicest possible way that the registrar should go ahead and see Theatre Sister about the case, and when he was out of earshot, asked in a placid voice: 'What's all this about you leaving, Kate?'

'Well, I am,' was all she could find to say.

'For some good reason?' He sounded very persuasive and she found herself saying:

'It seemed a good one.'

'But not any more,' he finished for her. 'You're off this evening? Good, we shall have dinner somewhere and you can tell me all about it.' And when she hesitated: 'Well, you can tell me, can't you? It's easy talking to a stranger—besides, I'm no gossip.' He didn't give her time to prevaricate. 'I'll wait for you at the entrance—about seven o'clock suit you?'

Katrina found herself looking forward to the

evening; it was quite true one could often tell things to a stranger that one wouldn't dream of discussing with one's nearest and dearest. Her mind shied away from the fact that he had described himself as a stranger, though. But why should he be anything else? She went off duty late because the accident case had gone to the theatre later than had been planned. He was in the I.C.U. when she enquired just before she left the ward, and likely to pull through. A marvellous job on the leg, Margaret Cross, the theatre Sister, told her enthusiastically; as for the arm, although it would never be the same again, it would be better than no arm at all. 'Quite a genius, our Dutch honorary,' she went on happily, 'and marvellous to work for. What's he like on the ward?'

'Very nice,' said Katrina sedately.

She wore the blue jersey again and spent time on her hair and face. The Professor had said somewhere quiet and she hoped she would do; in any case, she didn't much care. Life had gone sour on her and it was her own fault; she should have listened more carefully to Jack, then she could have stopped him from making his preposterous suggestion. If only he hadn't taken her to that Chinese place, if only . . . She reached the entrance and walked through the door, to find the Professor deep in conversation with Margaret. They both turned to look at her as she went towards them and Margaret said: 'Hullo—you look smashing, Kate, have a lovely evening.' She rolled fine blue eyes heavenwards. 'More than I shall! Bill and I are going to distemper the kitchen.'

'But think of the fun of being in your very own kitchen in a few weeks' time,' observed Katrina. She smiled at the Professor as she spoke and wished him a good evening rather sedately, wondering if she should have come after all; she didn't feel all that good company, and he might find her dull . . .

He seemed to have no doubts, at any rate; she was popped into the car and they were out of the forecourt before she had time to think up something to say. 'I said somewhere quiet,' he remarked placidly. 'How about the Waterside at Bray? Nice and peaceful by the river and there shouldn't be too many people there so early in the evening. They're keeping a table for us, but if there's somewhere else you'd prefer, do say so.'

Katrina didn't know whether to laugh or cry. 'It—it sounds lovely, but anywhere will do as long as it's not a Chinese restaurant.' Her voice was high and had a little shake in it.

'The reason for you leaving?' enquired the Professor, at his most tranquil.

'Yes, I suppose it is in a way.'

She waited for him to ask more questions, but he didn't, only embarked on a rambling small talk about nothing in particular and just sufficiently amusing to hold her attention.

By the time they reached Bray she was so soothed by it that she was ready and willing to pour out the whole miserable story, but he gave her no chance; she was seated at a table overlooking the river, given a drink and then the menu. With a little gentle prompting from her host she decided on *soufflé Eleonora*, followed by *filets de barbue au champagne* and obediently drank the excellent sherry she was offered. It was presently, when she had sampled these delights and rounded them off with a heavenly pudding, and the whole washed down by an excellent white wine, that the Professor paused in his light-hearted conversation.

'And now supposing that you tell me all about it, Katrina.'

'It'll bore you . . .'

'No,' and funnily enough she believed him.

It was difficult to begin, and she was still hesitating when he prompted: 'Why not start with the Chinese food?'

It all came pouring out, a frightful muddle of Jack Bentall, the disadvantages of being a big girl, sweet and sour pork and the utter stupidity of letting it be known that she was leaving to take up another post. 'In the Gulf, too,' she said bitterly. 'It's a part of the world I've never really wanted to visit.'

'Well, you don't have to go, you know,' observed the Professor in a soothing voice.

'No, but I've resigned, don't you see? I've no job—I'll have to find one, there's nothing else for it.'

A small smile tugged at the corners of the Professor's firm mouth. 'Yes, there is, but not just now, I think.'

Katrina opened her mouth to protest and thought better of it. He looked as placid as usual, but somehow she felt she would get nowhere if she started to argue with him. She said instead: 'I've been very silly.'

'Oh, no! If you had allowed—this—what is his name? Jack Bentall, to ride roughshod over you, telling you what to eat and arranging your life to suit himself, then you would have been a very silly girl. It was perhaps a little imaginative of you to get yourself a job in the Gulf, but it can always fall through at the last minute, you know.' He smiled at her. 'And now we won't talk about it any more. Are you on duty in the morning? Yes? Then I had better drive you back.'

And although she made one or two attempts to re-open the conversation, he skilfully prevented her.

It was a splendid evening, with a full moon and a sky crowded with stars, and when he advised her in a friendly fashion to forget her worries and enjoy the lovely night, she said quietly: 'I'm sorry, I'm being a bore. It is a lovely night—what a pity one can see so little of it from the nurses' home at Benedict's.'

'Not the pleasantest part of London,' conceded the Professor, 'but then the older hospitals so seldom are—it is the same in Holland, although the modern buildings are excellently sited.'

She would have liked to have learned more, but he was already turning into the forecourt. It was at the entrance, when she had thanked him for her evening and wished him good night, that he said matter-of-factly: 'I'm glad that you enjoyed it. I did. We have a good deal in common, and not only our size, Kate.'

She said a little shyly: 'Well, it is much nicer . . .' and paused, for the remark struck her as fatuous.

'In Friesland, which is my home land,' observed the Professor, 'both men and women are tall and well-built—you would go unnoticed there, Kate.' He gave a sudden crack of laughter. 'No, that's not true—you would never go unnoticed, Katrina.'

She looked at him, searching for a suitable answer to the quite unexpected compliment, but before she could think of anything to say, he had opened the door for her and she found herself inside, with the door shut firmly behind her.

It was two days before she saw him again. Uncle Ben came for his usual round, gave it his opinion that on the whole it might be a good thing if Katrina gave up her job at Benedicts. 'Otherwise you'll be here for the rest of your life,' he admonished her. 'You know how it is, you get into a rut and there you stay until you wake up to find that you're retiring next year . . .'

Katrina, who had been a little apprehensive about telling him her news, was relieved to hear this speech. 'Of course I'm not going to the Gulf,' she told him as he sat in her office drinking coffee before going on to the Women's Surgical. 'I thought I'd have a week or two at home and decide what to do.'

Uncle Ben gave her a thoughtful glance. 'Yes, you do that, my dear. You never know what may turn up.'

The Professor came early the following day, walking silently into the dressings room where Katrina was checking the sterile dressing packs. For a wonder it was fairly quiet on the ward;

moreover, she had both Julie and Moira on duty, which meant that she could do several small chores at her leisure. She had her back to the door as he went in and supposing it to be Julie, spoke without turning round.

'Ask Moira to go to coffee, will you, Julie and she can take Nurse Jeffs with her—when they come back send the others, we'll have coffee in the office.' She closed a drawer and opened another. 'Oh, and I'll take a look at Johnny Clark's dressing when it's down . . .'

'Good morning, Katrina,' said the Professor quietly, and she dropped the dressing pack she was holding and shot round to face him.

'Oh, it's you,' she observed, her usual serenity ruffled. 'Good morning. Did you want to see someone?'

'You. From your remarks I take it that you're not too busy to spare me ten minutes.'

She asked a little breathlessly: 'Oh, have you thought of something? I've been a bit worried, although Uncle Ben seems to think it's a good idea if I leave. I haven't told Mother yet and I haven't an idea what I'm going to do . . .'

He held the door wide for her to go past him. 'That is what I've come to see you about.'

'Yes, well . . .' She felt nervous and did her best to cover it up.

'I think I should say what I have to say first,' said the Professor blandly, and ushered her into her office, closing the door firmly behind him.

He looked so businesslike that Katrina didn't sit down behind her desk, but stood in front of it facing him. 'Have you heard of a job?' she asked hopefully.

He shook his head. 'I haven't made any attempt to look for one. If you will sit down, I will tell you what I have in mind.'

She sat, her hands clasped loosely in her lap, her head a little on one side, watching him. She wished he would sit himself, for he loomed enormous in the little room so that for once she wasn't so conscious of her own magnificent proportions. But he remained standing, leaning against the door, so that if anyone wanted to come in, they wouldn't be able to. He wasn't smiling either; it must be something which required serious discussion—she couldn't imagine what, but she was prepared to listen carefully: she was secretly worried about her future, although she had concealed her worry well enough from her friends; she was beginning to think that any likely solution would be welcome.

She gave him a questioning glance and he smiled a little. 'Would you consider marrying me?' asked Professor van Tellerinck.

Katrina's beautiful eyes goggled at him, her soft curving mouth fell open. 'Marry . . . ?' she began.

'I should like a wife,' went on the Professor, in much the tone of voice of one wishing for a new pair of shoes or the latest good book. 'I have considered it for some time, but until I met you I had not given it really serious thought.'

Katrina drew breath and uttered a sound which could have been anything at all, but she was ignored. 'I realise that we know very little about each other and in the normal course of events I would have suggested that we became engaged for several months so that we might remedy that, but since you find yourself—er—without employment and without definite ideas as to your future, it seems sensible to marry as soon as possible, don't you agree?' He didn't give her a chance to speak, but went on blandly: 'I suggest that we regard the first few months of marriage as a trial period. Will you marry me, Kate?'

She stared at him, her eyes enormous, her mouth still open. When she didn't answer, he prompted: 'Well—you don't answer . . .'

'I'm flabbergasted!'

His expression didn't alter, only his eyebrows rose a little so that she went pink. 'You're so surprised, then, Kate?'

'Yes—Oh, yes. I'm sorry, I didn't intend to be rude, only . . . well, I didn't like you very much when we met and I didn't think you liked me and I can't help wondering why . . . is it because I'm more your size?'

His eyes were almost hidden beneath their lids, but his smile was kind. 'I have never found you . . .' He stopped and began again. 'I had thought that you were beginning to like me just a little.'

'Well, yes, I am—I mean I do.' She swallowed and hurried on: 'But you don't love me.'

His voice was very placid. 'You are twenty-seven, Kate, and I am more than ten years older than you. Have we not reached an age where the first fine rapture of love is a little unlikely? It seems to me that a liking for the same things and a mutual regard for each other is more likely to make for a happy marriage.'

'Yes, I suppose so.' He was right, of course,

but it was hard to fling romance away without a backward glance. 'But do you like me—I mean enough to want to marry me?'

'Yes, Kate, I like you.' He sounded reassuringly friendly and normal, and quite suddenly the whole thing didn't seem preposterous at all.

'Yes, well ... if I could have time to think about it ...'

The Professor contrived to look wistful and worried at the same time.

'Now that is the difficulty. I have to go to Edinburgh—a series of lectures—in a month's time. It would be convenient if we could marry before then. We might have a few days' holiday in Scotland before returning to Holland.' He went on smoothly: 'And I'm sure you will agree with me that we should take our time in getting to know each other so that we may make sure of our feelings before we assume a deeper relationship. I have no wish to rush you into anything.'

He sounded a little old-fashioned, rather like a professor in fact, but Katrina didn't like him the less for that, she was inclined to be old-fashioned herself. If she did marry him she would need time to get adjusted to the idea although now, being honest with herself, she had to admit that she liked him; perhaps she had liked him all the time, she wasn't sure about that. They might even be very happy together in a mild kind of way; the wistful thought that he didn't expect more than that crossed her mind, but she dismissed it. 'I haven't even decided,' she said out loud.

'You have your days off tomorrow,' observed

the Professor, cutting into her musing. 'May I not drive you home?'

She searched his face. 'I don't know a thing about you,' she said.

'Soon told, but not now, I think. I'll tell you as we go.'

'Will you stay?' she asked him. 'Even if I . . . Perhaps I won't have made up my mind . . .'

'I should like to stay, if your mother has no objection.' He looked very relaxed and sure of himself, almost as though she had already decided. She was about to utter another disclaimer when the telephone shrilled, and she lifted the receiver.

'It's for you,' she said, and sat silent while he listened, gave terse instructions and then put the receiver down. 'I have to go, I'll see you later.'

She was left alone, wondering what later meant, still bemused.

She should have been off duty that evening, but the case the Professor had been called away to see was admitted to the ward just before dinner time and went to theatre an hour later. Intensive Care handed him back to the ward about four o'clock and he was still far too ill for her to go off duty; Moira was on that evening, but Katrina, who would have handed over to Julie quite happily, hesitated to leave him with her. She decided to stay until the night staff came on at half past eight. She wasn't doing anything anyway she told herself, there had been no sight of the Professor either.

In this she was proved wrong, for he turned up around six o'clock to take a look at his patient. 'A very nasty perforated ulcer,' he observed, 'but he should do. Who is looking after him?'

'I am,' said Katrina, 'just until the night staff come on duty.'

He didn't waste time asking questions, only nodded. 'Well, we'll have a meal,' he told her. 'Somewhere close by, though. There's a pub down the street, isn't there? The Lamb and Fleece. It's not five minutes' walk away, we could have something in the basket.'

Katrina, whose dinner had been sketchy, agreed at once. 'I'm famished,' she told him, and then added hesitantly: 'I meant to drive down this evening, but it'll be too late . . .'

'I'd rather not go until the morning; suppose we leave about eight o'clock? Could you manage that? Sir Benjamin isn't taking over until midnight and anything could happen between now and then.'

She nodded. 'Yes, of course. I'll be ready at eight. Are you sure you want to go out this evening? I'm not off until around nine o'clock.'

His eyes searched her face sleepily. 'You should have been off for the evening?'

'Well, yes, but I thought I'd stay on and give a hand for a while . . .'

He nodded, taking it for granted that she forfeited her free time willingly. 'Shall we say a quarter past nine, then? Put a coat on over your uniform, no one will notice.'

Katrina was tired by the time they met and although she had tidied herself she hadn't bothered much with make-up, only flung a coat on as he had suggested. As she glanced at herself in the mirror in her room, ready to leave, she thought it was a good opportunity for him to see what she looked like when she was weary and careless of her appearance. And far too tired to give a thought to his proposals as to her future. If he started on that, she told herself as she ran down the stairs, she would most likely turn the whole thing down flat.

The Professor was too clever for that; he walked her to the pub, found a small table in its crowded saloon bar, put a glass of sherry before her, refreshed himself with beer and offered the menu.

The food was homely; they spent a few minutes debating the merits of beans and fried eggs or fish and chips in a basket, and presently Katrina settled for the fish and chips and her companion ordered the same, and while they were waiting for it, embarked upon an account of the case that morning. He could be amusing as well as interesting; they passed from that to a general survey of surgery and from that to some lighthearted reminiscences of his student days. They followed their supper with cups of coffee and they were still sitting over them when closing time was called.

As they strolled the short distance back to Benedict's they were for the most part silent. Pleasantly silent, thought Katrina, like two old friends who didn't have to talk unless they wanted to. They were just inside the door when the night porter came to meet them. 'I was just going to buzz you, sir—you're wanted in the Accident Room.'

The Professor's goodnight had been brisk, almost businesslike; his crisp: 'Eight o'clock in the car park' was equally so. Katrina flung some clothes into a case before she got into bed and remembered that she hadn't telephoned her mother. Well, it was too late now, and her parent, thank heaven, wasn't a woman to fuss over unexpected guests.

Contrary to her expectations she went to sleep the moment her head touched the pillow, and she didn't wake until her alarm clock roused her.

She took longer than usual dressing; it was going to be a lovely day, that was obvious even at such an early hour in the heart of London. She decided to wear an Italian knitted suit in a shade of almond green and her new Raynes shoes. The outfit called for extra care with her hair and face, so that there was barely time to make a cup of tea in the tiny pantry at the end of the corridor before she left.

And even though she was punctual to the minute, the Professor was there before her, leaning against the Bentley's gleaming hood, lost in contemplation of the chimney pots on the opposite side of the street. He came to meet her as soon as he saw her, however, took her case and put it in the trunk and opened the car door.

'You look nice,' he told her. 'It's going to be a beautiful day, too. Have you breakfasted? Do say no, because I haven't.'

She laughed, 'I haven't either.'

'We'll use the A3 and then stop at the Hog's Back on the other side of Guildford—the A31, isn't it?'

'Yes, I forgot to telephone Mother. She won't mind in the least, you may have to take pot luck for lunch.'

They breakfasted with splendid appetites and set off again through a perfect April morning, and once they had passed Farnham and were racing along the A31 towards the Alton round-about and Alresford, Katrina broke their companionable silence: 'You were going to tell me something about yourself,' she suggested.

'Ah, yes. Where to begin? I live in the country, to the north of Leiden, but my family came from Friesland originally, a small village not so far from Leeuwarden. I have a housekeeper and a houseman—an elderly couple who look after things for me. I'm away a good deal; I have beds in Leiden hospitals as well as in den Haag and Amsterdam. I have no family.'

She turned her head to look at him. 'No father or mother?'

His profile was all at once bleak. 'They—died a month or so before the war ended.'

She had seen the bleakness. 'Died?' she asked softly.

'They were shot by the Germans for helping someone to escape.'

She caught at his sleeve with a hand. 'Oh, Raf, how terrible, and how sad! Do you remember them at all?'

'Oh, yes. I was getting on for four years old. Caspel and his wife—they are with me still—took me to Friesland, walking all the way, to my grandparents who had a house there. It was my home until they died and in the meantime my father's property was restored to me. Once I had qualified I went to live there.'

'All alone,' said Katrina in a sad voice.

'Quite alone, Kate.'

'Oh, I'm sorry,' she told him, 'though what's the good of being sorry? But you must feel proud too, to have had such a Father and Mother, bearing their name.' Her lovely eyes filled with tears. 'You were such a little boy . . .'

'Don't forget that at least I had grandparents, many children had no one at all.'

'Yes, but now you're all alone.'

'Don't tempt me to use that as an argument for you to marry me, Kate.'

'Oh, I hadn't thought of that. But you wouldn't would you?'

'No. How about stopping for a coffee?'

It was while they were drinking it that she asked: 'Just supposing I did marry you, would you like me to go on working—a lot of wives do.'

His eyes danced with amusement beneath their heavy lids but he answered seriously enough. 'Oh, I don't think so. I've plenty for two and I'm sure you'll find things to do around the house, and there's the garden. I have a number of friends too; there would be the occasional dinner party and function to attend.'

'Do you have a secretary or a receptionist?'

'At my consulting rooms, yes, but I can always do well with help at home—most of the mail goes there, you see, and it does pile up.'

Katrina brightened at the prospect of making herself useful, and he added: 'I shall enjoy having company, Kate—someone I can talk to and discuss the day's work with, someone, moreover, who will understand what I'm talking about.'

She looked up and caught his eyes looking at her so intently that she said quite sharply: 'I haven't made up my mind . . .'

She changed it a dozen times during the rest of their journey. When Sherborne came in sight at last she still couldn't make up her mind; childishly, she hoped that there would be some omen to make it up for her. It would have to be soon, too. She tried to imagine what it would be like if she did refuse and chose not to see Raf ever again, and had to admit that she wouldn't like it at all. He grew on one, she mused, sitting silent beside him, in a placid kind of way, only every now and then he wasn't placid at all.

CHAPTER FOUR

IT wasn't one of Sherborne's busy days. The Professor drove the Bentley slowly through the town, turned down a side street, skirted the boys' school and gentled the big car into the quiet little backwater where Katrina lived.

The house looked charming, its garden a riot of colour, its latticed windows open. They went up the flagged path side by side, and the door was found open before they reached it.

'Darling, what a lovely surprise!' exclaimed Mrs Bennett happily, 'and Raf too.' She nodded her head in a satisfied way. 'You'll stay, of course.' And then, with all the disconcerting simplicity of a child: 'Why?'

'Mother dear,' began Katrina, and stopped, not quite sure how to go on, but the Professor didn't beat about the bush.

'I've asked Katrina to marry me,' he said matter-of-factly, 'and she thought she would like to come home and think about it.'

'Splendid!' Mrs Bennett beamed at him, 'I was only thinking the other day that really Katrina should be the first to marry, being the eldest, you know.' She waved an arm. 'Come in, my dears, and tell me all about it—I do love a wedding. It's a cold lunch, will you mind? And Raf can have the guest room . . .'

Ten minutes later, over their sherry, Mrs

Bennett asked: 'Is it to be a white wedding, Kate? Satin, dear, cut very simply; you've such a good figure.' She turned to the Professor. 'Hasn't she, Raf?'

Katrina went pink. 'Mother, I've not said I'll get married yet . . .' She glanced at Raf and saw the twinkle in his eyes and suddenly she didn't feel awkward any more. Not even when he agreed with her mother with a good deal of warmth.

'Would you like to be married in satin?' he asked interestedly.

Katrina thought for a minute. 'Well, neither of us have large families and your friends won't want to come all this way, will they? I think it should be quiet; just us and Uncle Ben and—and anyone you wanted to ask.' The pink which hadn't quite subsided glowed crimson. 'Not that I've said . . .'

'No, no,' agreed the Professor soothingly, 'it was merely a hypothetical question.'

Mrs Bennett had picked up some knitting. 'That would be nice,' she mused. 'We could come back here for a luncheon party afterwards. Where will you live?'

'My home and my work are in Holland,' explained the Professor, his voice placid, 'but I do come to England very frequently and of course Kate would come with me.'

'It's all so suitable.' She stopped knitting to look at them both in turn. 'Well, Kate darling, you can sit in the garden after lunch and make your mind up while I show Raf the Abbey.'

Which wasn't quite what Katrina had intended, but perhaps it wasn't such a bad idea after all, for it was very peaceful sitting in one of the elderly deck chairs, with Mrs Mogg, the family cat, curled up on her lap. Left to herself after casual goodbyes from her mother and the Professor, Katrina relaxed. She relaxed so well that she went to sleep in no time at all.

When she woke up, an hour later, it was to find the Professor sitting on the chopping block, facing her, and to her great surprise, although she hadn't given a thought to her problem, it seemed to have solved itself while she was sleeping, because she said without any hesitation at all:

'Yes, of course I'll marry you, Raf, that's if you still want me to.'

He smiled faintly. 'Yes, I want you to, Kate.' He got to his feet and caught hold of her hands and pulled her up. 'Shall we go and tell your mother? She's getting the tea and sent me to find you, but I hadn't the heart to wake you up.'

'I wasn't snoring?'

He tucked a hand under her arm. 'Not so that you'd notice. I liked the Abbey, do you suppose we could be married in one of the chapels?'

'I don't see why not. I mean, with Father having been there ... and we know everyone quite well. I'd like that if you would.'

They went in through the side door and met Mrs Bennett with the teapot in her hand. 'We'll have a cup now,' she told them. 'The other two will be home at five o'clock, we can have another cup with them.' She threw Katrina a sharp glance. 'So you've decided,' she declared happily. And when Katrina looked surprised: 'Well, you wouldn't be walking arm-in-arm otherwise, would you?' she observed.

The rest of the day passed in a pleasant dream, with Ruth and Jane showering congratulations on them both, and plunging at once into the vital question of what they should wear at the wedding. The Professor didn't say much, only when there was a pause in the conversation, suggested diffidently that he and Katrina might stroll round and see whoever it was they had to see about the licence, and when that had been done, settled with the least possible fuss by Raf, they went on walking through the quiet little town and she discovered that he had a solution, offered in the most matter-of-fact way, to each and every of her small doubts and problems. It was almost as though he had planned everything days before and had an answer ready for any contingency. But that was absurd, she told herself.

They wandered back presently to drink the champagne Raf had thoughtfully brought with him in the car, and eat the rather special dinner Mrs Bennett and Mary had conjured up, and later, just as she was falling asleep, Katrina was suddenly sure that she was doing the right thing. Unexpected and rather sudden, but right. She turned over and went to sleep on the thought.

She and Raf went for a walk before breakfast the following day—a suggestion he had made the previous evening. 'So that we can get the date settled,' he had suggested placidly, 'and the time . . .'

They agreed on ten o'clock in the morning, in three weeks' time; they could return to her home for an hour after the wedding and then leave for

Scotland, spending a night on the way. 'We'll be there for a week, at least. I shall be lecturing for that time. I thought that if you would like to, we might spend a few days travelling around before we go back to Holland.'

Katrina agreed happily; it would give them a chance to get used to each other and time to learn about his home and way of life. A busy one, by all accounts, but he hadn't told her much so far.

'Do you go to Friesland often?' she wanted to know.

'Oh, frequently—the farm is managed by a remote cousin of mine, but I like to go there as often as I can.' He turned to smile at her. 'You like farming?'

'I don't know a great deal about it, but I'm sure I shall love it. Is there a garden?' she added.

'Yes, a very pleasant one—you will be able to potter there as much as you like.'

'And your home? What's it like?'

'Oh, old and square with a steep tiled roof—like so many other Dutch houses.'

She had to be content with that; Raf started talking about something else and she found it impossible, without being downright rude, to ask more questions.

It was after breakfast when she had supposed him safely telephoning someone or other, and had slipped into the garden to hang the washing on the carefully concealed line behind the lilac bushes, that he came to join her. She threw him a glance over her shoulder and spoke first.

'Mother and Ruth and Jane are too small,' she explained matter-of-factly, 'so when I'm home I always do it.' She tossed a sheet over the line with effortless grace and stretched her magnificent proportions to peg it.

Raf stood watching her. 'Penthesilea,' he murmured.

Katrina frowned, shook out a pillow case and then said smugly: 'I know—Queen of the Amazons, wasn't she? Came to a sticky end, too.'

'I wasn't thinking of her end,' observed the Professor mildly, so really, Katrina told herself crossly, there was no reason why she should blush. She made a great work of pegging a tablecloth and hurried on: 'Father was interested in mythology; he read Latin and Greek like I read the *Telegraph*, he used to let me sit with him as long as I didn't disturb him—over the years I worked my way through Beeton's Classical Dictionary.'

'Do you read Greek and Latin as well?'

She picked up the laundry basket and he took it from her. 'Heavens, no, but it was much more exciting than Grimm's Fairy Tales.' And when he laughed: 'I suppose you do . . .?'

He sounded almost apologetic. 'Well, yes, I do—not avidly, though: I shan't object to you interrupting me when I do.'

He gave her a hard stare and she looked back at him, faintly bewildered by it. It was like having a spell cast over one, she thought childishly, and then, even more bewildered, a spell she didn't mind about. But before she could think about it he said in an ordinary voice:

'I wondered if we might dine out this evening—all of us; Ruth's fiancé and Jane's current boy-friend and your mother, naturally.'

'That would be fun. Where?'

'Sir Benjamin told me of a good place at Win-canton—Holbrook House.'

'Oh, lovely! We've been there once or twice—birthdays and that sort of thing.'

'Would it be an idea if we went round to see your vicar, Mr Thomas?—he's not married, I understand—to make up the numbers?'

He sounded as if he had just thought of it, but later, making beds, Katrina wondered if he hadn't laid his plans beforehand, knowing quite well that everyone would fall in with them as long as he proposed them at the right time. Would it be like that when they were married? she wondered uneasily, and then rejected the idea, he had a caustic tongue upon occasion, but on the whole he was a placid man, not easily put out—or put upon, she added thoughtfully.

Mr Thomas would be delighted. They took the opportunity to discuss the details of the wedding while they were there and then strolled into the town's main street, looking at the shop windows. It was Katrina who deliberately didn't look in the jeweller's; an engagement ring hadn't been men-tioned—perhaps she wasn't to have one. She looked away as they reached the best one in town, but Raf caught her hand and stopped her. 'I'll bring the ring with me,' he told her. 'It's been in the family for quite some time—a little old-fashioned, but I hope you won't mind.'

She didn't know how her eyes sparkled. 'Oh—how nice! I shall love it. When are you going back to Holland?'

'Tomorrow evening—I've some lectures to

give, but I'll be back within a week. I promised
Sir Benjamin that I'd give him a hand with that
arterial graft—he hasn't quite decided whether to
do a thrombo-endarterectomy and core out the
lining . . .'

'Oh, you're talking about Mr Parsons who came
in yesterday—does it have to be surgery?'

'Oh, yes, I'm afraid so . . .' The talk turned to
surgery in general and kept them occupied until
they reached home once more. Not quite the kind
of conversation one would have expected between
two newly engaged people, perhaps, and as they
entered the house Raf paused in the doorway to
say: 'I teased you once—when we met—because
we talked about the weather, and now I have
been boring on for hours about something you
must be only too glad to escape once in a while.'

Katrina eyed him gravely. 'Usually I am, but I
enjoyed it, really I did.' She hesitated. 'You don't
know me very well, Raf. I'm not—not frivolous, I
mean, I'm not very amusing company and I'm
not witty or anything like that. I like clothes, but
I don't worry about them, if you know what I
mean. I can cook and sew and do the washing if
the machine breaks down, but I haven't any—
any . . .'

'Parlour tricks? My dear, I've seen all of those.
I think you may rest assured that we shall suit
very well' He grinned wickedly. 'I hope at any
rate that you will find me a shade better than the
Gulf!'

Katrina chuckled. 'Wasn't I a fool? The things
one says when one is unprepared!'

They spent the afternoon in the garden, Raf

mowing the lawn with beautiful precision while Katrina weeded under her mother's eye. Mrs Bennett had started off weeding too, but had declared herself tired to death and made herself comfortable in a deck chair, opening an eye every now and then to point out the odd groundsel or blade of grass which her daughter had overlooked. But presently she dropped off to sleep and the Professor, finished with his mowing, made short work of the rest of the weeds, pulled Katrina to her feet and suggested that they should sit under the lilacs at the end of the garden. It was warm there, sheltered from the wind, and they didn't bother to talk much. Katrina, covertly eyeing her companion, stretched out beside her with his eyes closed, found it somehow reassuring that they could be together and not need to talk.

'You're very restful,' said the Professor suddenly, and opened an eye. 'When I've finished my lecturing in Edinburgh, shall we go to the west coast? A small place called Ledaig, there's a delightful hotel there—you cross a bridge to reach it; it's on an island only a short distance from the shore. I think you might like it, Kate. I was there a couple of years ago and I enjoyed it enormously. No cinema or dancing or shops, just fields and the sea and animals and delicious food. If we need the bright lights Oban is no distance away.'

'It sounds super, and I don't suppose I'll need any bright lights. I'll have time to read and look at the birds. Do you fish?'

'Yes, but I won't—it's rather dull for the non-fisher.'

'I'm willing to learn, but I don't think I'd like the worms and hooks.'

He smiled up at her. 'I won't fish. I shall probably lie down all day doing absolutely nothing.'

'Is that all the holiday you'll get this year?'

'Good lord, no—I snatch a day here and a day there and most weekends.'

'But you have hospital rounds,' she persisted, 'and a practice?'

'Oh, yes, of course. I'm afraid I have rather a full day's work, but being a nurse you'll understand that—and I'm often away from home.'

'Your lectures ... Do you visit interesting places?' She was angry with herself for saying that; it sounded as though she wanted to go too. So she added with a touch of pettishness: 'That sounds as though I want to go too, but I don't.'

'What a pity.' His tone was light, so she wasn't sure if he were joking or meant it. She asked hastily: 'Do you fly?'

'Always, unless it's in Holland or perhaps Belgium.'

Katrina seemed unable to stop the questions tripping off her tongue.

'Are you important?' she asked.

'My dear girl, what is importance? A housewife is important in her kitchen, but only because she knows what to do there—if I'm important, which I doubt, it's because I know what to do with a scalpel when I'm handed one.'

She wasn't getting anywhere; she had asked several questions and the answers had been clear and concise and had told her virtually nothing.

She said crossly: 'Now if Father were alive he would ask you all sorts of questions and you'd answer . . .'

'How much do I earn and can I support you in a manner to which you are accustomed? Isn't that right? Well, my dear, I have sufficient to do that . . .'

'Now you've made me sound like a prying harpy!'

Raf's huge shoulders shook. 'My dear Kate, have you any idea what exactly a harpy is?'

'Well, no—I don't think I have . . .'

'A fabulous winged monster, quite ravenous and filthy dirty, with the body of a woman, a face pale from hunger, and large wings. Somehow you don't quite fit the bill.'

Katrina got slowly to her feet. 'The trouble is,' she said thoughtfully, 'I'm never sure when to take you seriously.'

The dinner party was a resounding success; the hotel had at one time been a country house set in charming parkland and the owners had managed to keep its original atmosphere, merely adding good food and excellent service. Katrina, who had dug deep into the old oak clothes closet in her room, had found a cotton voile dress in tawny colours which she had had for at least two years and had intended to throw away, to discover when she tried it on that it was undeniably becoming and to all but the very discerning, quite fashionable. At any rate the Professor had declared that she had looked charming, adding with a decided twinkle in his eyes that he knew very little about girls' clothes: 'Although I must say that some fashions do seem rather peculiar.'

Katrina, pushing a comb into her hair, looked at him in the mirror. 'I expect you've had a lot of girl-friends,' she said.

The twinkle became a gleam. 'Oh, naturally—one must have company from time to time,' he explained, and smiled with great charm.

Katrina tugged the comb out and stuck it in again rather painfully. 'Well, you won't need them any more, you'll have me,' she reminded him with something of a snap.

'Yes, I had thought of that,' said the Professor placidly. 'That comb looked very nice where it was before, why didn't you leave it there?'

He took it gently out again and slid it expertly into its original place, then bent to kiss her cheek. 'I never asked any of the other girl-friends to marry me,' he told her gently.

Katrina enjoyed her evening very much after that.

They went back to London early the next morning because Katrina was on duty after one o'clock dinner. Usually she didn't mind too much, getting back into uniform and plunging back into the hustle and bustle of a big ward, but today, for some reason, she did. Perhaps because she wouldn't see Raf for a few days. She hadn't seen much of him at the hospital, but she had known that he was around somewhere and that he might pop in. It struck her that she had looked forward to their unexpected meetings. And anyone would think, she mused, sitting quietly beside him as they drove back, that I was never going to see him again, whereas in a couple of weeks I shall see him every day ... She went pink at the idea, and Raf, throwing her a quick sidelong glance, asked with interest: 'What are you blushing about, Kate?' He added thoughtfully: 'I've not said anything—I wasn't even thinking . . .'

Katrina giggled. 'Don't be absurd—and you don't have to sound aggrieved, because you never are. I—I was just thinking that I'd see more of you after we're married.'

His fine mouth quivered. 'It would be rather extraordinary if you didn't. But I must warn you, Kate, that I am a busy man, and if the day's gone badly, an ill-tempered one too.'

'In which case I shall go somewhere quiet with a good book,' said Kate.

They stopped for lunch at the Castle in Sunbury and he delivered her neatly to the nurses' home door with half an hour to spare. There were plenty of people about; she supposed that was why he parted from her with a casual: 'I'll see you in a few days, Kate,' and a wave as he drove off.

It seemed the right moment to discount the fiction of her job in the Gulf; she had only to tell one or two friends, pass the news on to Julie during the afternoon's work and ask for an interview at the office and by teatime the entire hospital knew that she was the lucky girl who was going to marry the handsome Dutchman that the unattached female staff had secretly hoped to capture for themselves. Inevitably, Jack bearded her in her office as she wrote the report that evening.

'That was a pack of lies you told me,' he began, gobbling with indignation.

Katrina held her pen poised over the Cardex. She looked down demurely and murmured: 'I had no idea when I told you about the job in the Gulf that I was going to marry Professor van Tellerinck.' Which was perfectly true. 'It all happened rather suddenly.'

'You can say that again—he's only been an honorary consultant for a few weeks.' His eyes narrowed. 'I suppose he's filthy rich?'

Katrina wrote a few words. 'You're being very rude—and I might add that it's none of your business.'

She wrote busily and after a moment or two he grunted something under his breath and went away. She finished her report and then, with five minutes to spare until the night staff came on duty, sat back to think. Jack hadn't worried her at all and she didn't give him a second thought, but a small niggling idea at the back of her head needed to be brought out into the open and aired. Was Raf rich, and how was she to find out anyway? He had always parried her questions very smoothly when she had asked him, and was it quite the done thing for a girl to ask her future husband what his income was? She supposed it was; in these hard times it was essential that they knew exactly what they were letting themselves in for. He had assured her that he had enough money to provide for her and at the time the answer had contented her; she wasn't greedy or extravagant and she was a good manager, she had no doubt at all that she would be able to manage very well with whatever he gave her for the house-hold expenses. She frowned and pushed her cap back on her head. That wasn't quite it; if he were a very rich man—and after all, he did run a Bentley—she wasn't sure that she would have said she would marry him, but she had, and it was too late to go back on her promise now. Anyway, she admitted, she didn't want to; Raf was much much nicer than she had thought he would be. Besides, she was fast reaching the conclusion that being with someone you liked and trusted was far more comfortable than loving someone to distraction and not being quite sure of him. She went to bed and slept dreamlessly after an uproarious hour with her friends, discussing wedding clothes.

She had told herself that she wouldn't buy any-thing at all until Raf came again, but the next day, with an afternoon off duty, it seemed a pity not to at least do a little window shopping. Rosina, the junior theatre Sister, and Delia, in charge of the Accident Room, were both off duty too, and the three of them took a bus to Regent Street where Katrina bought a pair of strappy sandals at Raynes in champagne kid and a leg-horn hat swathed with a chiffon scarf in a rich cream. A most sensible beginning to the buying of wedding clothes, she was assured by her friends, and back in her room, with the hat poised on top of her rich brown hair, she was in-clined to agree with them. She would have to find a suit or a dress which would go with it, but it would have to be something she could wear later.

She was on duty all day for the next two days so that shopping was out of the question, but on the day after that she was to have a morning off; she had some hours owing to her and both staff nurses on duty, so she had the whole morning free until one o'clock.

She went out immediately after breakfast and began painstakingly to search. Several times she found something which she liked and each time the size was wrong, so she was forced to reject them in turn. She was beginning to lose heart when she found exactly what she wanted—a sleeveless dress and little jacket in a thick slub silk, its colour an exact match of the chiffon in the hat. What was more, it fitted. Katrina, studying herself carefully in the pier glass, beamed at the sales lady, who beamed back and forgot to be aloof. 'Modom is a big girl,' she observed in a voice of ultra-refinement, 'but Modom has the figure to carry off the beautiful lines of the dress—such an exquisite cut . . .'

The price was exquisite too; Katrina had come prepared to be extravagant, but this was ridiculous. She got out her cheque book and paid without protest.

It had all taken a long time, of course. She was tearing across the forecourt, intent on getting to her room, when she ran full tilt into Raf. A man of lesser bulk might have been bowled over, but all he did was to clamp her round the waist, take her dress box from her and remark: 'Shopping, I see. The wedding dress, I hope? Where can we go for a moment?'

'Nowhere,' said Katrina, a little breathless and not altogether from hurrying either. 'I mean, I'm on duty in twenty minutes—and do take care of that box,' and then: 'How nice to see you.'

'I should have said that first, shouldn't I? I know somewhere we can go.'

He hurried her through the entrance, across the hall and into a wide corridor where she did her best to come to a halt; a quite useless effort anyway, although she did protest in a hissing whisper as he opened a door. 'Raf, you can't—not in here—it's where the consultants come . . .'

'I'm a consultant, aren't I? And there's no one here, is there?' He smiled at her in his sleepy fashion. 'Don't fuss, Kate.' He put the box down on the old-fashioned central table, and still holding her by the arm, fished a box out of a pocket. 'Open it,' he suggested.

She blinked at the ring inside—a great sapphire, flanked by smaller ones on either side and all three surrounded by rose diamonds. 'My goodness!' gasped Katrina. 'It's—it's absolutely super—I'll never dare to wear it!'

For answer Raf took the ring from her and slipped it on her finger, where it looked exactly right; what was more, it fitted.

Katrina held up her hand and looked at the jewel from every angle. 'It's magnificent—oh, I'll take such care of it! Thank you very much, Raf.'

She looked at him a little uncertainly and he read her thoughts unerringly. 'Shall we not kiss and seal our pact?' he suggested in such a matter-of-fact voice that she forgot to feel awkward and flung her arms round his neck and kissed him with the spontaneous pleasure of a child. She drew back almost at once; his kiss had been brief and friendly, like hundreds of other kisses from

hundreds of other people; there was no reason
why she should have felt unhappy about it, but
she did, and made haste to cover it up.

'So sorry,' she told him brightly. 'I got carried
away—it must be the effect of having sapphires
offered to one before lunch,' and before he could
answer: 'That reminds me—I've about five
minutes in which to change and get on duty—I
simply have to go.'

It was more than five minutes, but it wasn't
long enough for her to brood over his cool re-
ception of her kiss; she'd think about that later. It
was much later when she finally left the ward.
The afternoon and evening had proved even
busier than usual, and Uncle Ben had been to see
a new case of his, so had Jack Bentall and a variety of other people—path lab. technicians, the
lady from C.S.R., fussing about some packs
which had gone astray, the dietetician, who
wasted a lot of valuable time fretting over
steamed fish. Katrina, who had her mind on
other things, wished her and her fish a thousand
miles away.

She said good night thankfully to the night
staff and went yawning down the stairs. She had
intended to try on the new outfit, but now she
was tired, more so because she was hungry too.
She was rounding the dark corner at the bottom
when she bumped into something very solid,
Raf's massive waistcoated chest, and she was so
delighted that she put out a hand and grabbed at
it, babbling, 'Oh, I'm so glad . . . I wasn't looking, I'm sorry,' and then, like a child: 'I'm tired!'

Just for a moment he held her close. 'Go and

get your coat, we're going to your uncle's—you
need a stiff drink and something decent to eat and
half an hour to unwind.'

It was nice to have someone arranging everything for her, but she protested all the same: 'I'm
a bit bad-tempered too—not fit company.'

'Do as I say,' said Raf quietly, and dis-
entangled her from his chest with kind impersonal hands, so that she said: 'Very well,' at
once and hurried to her room. She had irritated
him, whining about being tired and then clinging
to him like a leech. She must be careful never to
do that again . . .

Uncle Ben and Aunt Lucy were so kind. The
ring was admired while Raf got them all drinks,
and when she had relaxed under the influence of
the Madeira he had given her, they sat down to
supper; one of Katrina's aunt's light-as-air ome-
lettes and a bowl of salad. They sat for a short
while afterwards, talking, and Katrina became
aware that Raf was rather quiet; perhaps he was
annoyed because she had sprawled all over his
waistcoat and moaned about being tired, perhaps
he was having second thoughts about marrying
her.

It was a relief to hear him presently, discussing
the wedding with Uncle Ben. She listened un-
ashamedly while Aunt Lucy rambled on happily
about white satin and orange blossom, although
Katrina had pointed out to her several times that
for the bride to float down the aisle in all the tra-
ditional wedding finery with barely a dozen
people in the church to admire her seemed a bit
foolish. She caught Raf's eye presently and they

got up to go, and although he said very little on the short drive back, he kissed her lightly as they said good night and urged her to sleep well in a kind voice. In bed, on the point of sleep, she remembered that he hadn't said when they were to meet again.

CHAPTER FIVE

THE next two weeks went in a flash. Katrina, caught up in the business of handing over the ward to Julie, had no time to do more than smile and murmur at Raf when he came, either alone or with Uncle Ben to see their patients. True, they had managed to have dinner together twice before Raf went back to Holland, but they had talked about the wedding in a rather businesslike way, getting the times right, checking the travelling arrangements, and when he had said goodbye and gone, she wished with all her heart that she could have seen more of him; it would have made the wedding day seem more real. But there was no time to waste upon her vague doubts; she smothered them with a bout of shopping and then went home for her last days off before she left Benedict's for good.

Her mother welcomed her with open arms and a list of things to be done or decided upon. It was to be a very small wedding, but nonetheless Mrs Bennett had consoled herself for the lack of satin and orange blossom by arranging for an elegant luncheon party after the ceremony, and the purchase of a decidedly becoming outfit for the occasion. Katrina, who hadn't got around to thinking about wedding cakes and flowers, agreed to everything, surprised to hear that Raf had sent a case of champagne from London and that the flowers were already ordered. So that was why he had stopped on their way back from dinner and studied a florist's window so carefully, asking her if she liked roses, and how charming lilies of the valley were. To her great astonishment too, he had brought with him on that same evening, a pocket full of wedding rings, because, as he had pointed out, there was no chance of them going to a jeweller's and choosing one. She had decided on a plain gold one and rather shyly asked if she might give him one as well. He already wore a heavy signet ring and she hadn't been sure if he would like the idea, but he agreed readily, scooped the rings back into a careless heap, and promised her lightly that he wouldn't forget to bring them with him.

Her mother had given her a Gucci travelling case for a present, and Ruth and Jane had contributed a matching beauty case. Katrina spent a good deal of time packing these, for she was to leave Benedict's the day before she was to be married, which left precious little time. Indeed, her mother, sitting on the bed with her sisters, watching her fold her new outfits, bemoaned the fact at some length. 'No hairdresser, and no time for a manicure or something for your face . . .'

Katrina flew to the dressing table. 'Have I got spots?' she demanded.

'No, dear, of course not, you have a lovely skin and such pretty hair too . . . it's just that you seem to be being pitchforked into marriage with barely a good night's sleep as preparation.'

Katrina gave up looking for the mythical spot and went to hug her mother. 'Darling, don't worry, I'll have clean nails and a powdered nose, and it's only a very small affair, you know, Raf's only got a couple of his friends coming—I haven't even met them, and there'll be ten of us for lunch, no more. Besides, we have to leave by two o'clock.'

'Will you have time to come and see us before you go over to Holland?'

'I don't think so; Raf's got a full programme ahead of him—lectures, you know, but he's coming over to London in about six weeks and I'm to come too and we'll come and see you then.'

'Yes, dear. Katrina, I do hope . . .'

'We're going to be very happy,' said Katrina firmly.

It was surely wedding day weather, thought Katrina, creeping from her bed very early to peer out at the bright May morning. She glanced at her wedding hat, lying in splendour on the table under the window, and then jumped back into bed as she heard feet on the stairs.

'I thought I heard you up, Miss Kate,' said Mary severely. 'Don't you know better than to get out of bed before your breakfast on your wedding day. Now drink up this nice cup of tea and I'll be up in no time with a good nourishing meal.'

Just as though Raf intends to starve me for the rest of my life, thought Katrina, giggling, and then stopped because this really was her wedding day and she ought to be serious about it. It was too late now to wonder if she had done the right thing. Perhaps she hadn't; she was marrying Raf for several good reasons, but none of the usual ones; she admired and respected him, though, and that was surely important, and he was just about the handsomest man she had ever set eyes on; and she liked being with him. She hoped that he felt the same towards her, because if he did, they would probably make a success of their life together. All the same, marriage was a big risk . . .

Raf appeared to have no such doubts. As Katrina went into the Abbey and reached the little side chapel, he turned to look at her, his face calm and very assured so that at the sight of him, her mouth curved into a smile. Perhaps it wasn't quite the thing to think about clothes in church, but she knew that she looked her best and very feminine, despite the fact that she towered over Uncle Ben. She clutched the exquisite bouquet rather more tightly and glanced down at it: creamy roses, lilies of the valley, delicate pink orchids and carnations—all the flowers she had imagined, and admired. It was nice to think he had remembered and taken the trouble to get them.

There was a tall man standing beside Raf; the best man she hadn't met, and just beyond him, two more men, big and burly, faultlessly turned out, going elegantly grey at the temples, as self-assured as Raf. There were three youngish women there too, smartly dressed. Wives, thought Katrina; let's hope there's enough lunch—and why didn't Raf let us know?

She glanced at him and saw that he was looking at her with a half smile, probably guessing her thoughts. She looked at him gravely then; she was here to get married and anything else, for the moment, didn't matter.

The ceremony was very short. She hadn't really realised that it was all over before they had signed the register and she was walking out of the Abbey doors, the organ booming triumphantly in the empty Abbey and her hand tucked into Raf's arm. The bells were ringing too and she glanced at him in surprise. 'Because you are your father's daughter,' he said softly, 'they wanted to do it.'

They started down the path towards the Bentley and for a moment her steps faltered. 'Oh, Raf, how kind . . .' her voice shook a little because she had loved her father very much, and Raf glanced down at her face.

'I thought you were going to bawl me out for bringing unexpected guests,' he said cheerfully, and made her laugh. 'Your mother knew—I told her last night.'

'You telephoned?'

'I called, but you were already in bed.'

Someone was holding the car door open and she got in. 'Oh, why didn't you wake me?' she wanted to know. 'There were lots of things I wanted to say . . .'

He turned to look at her before he started the engine. 'And all the time in the world to say them, Kate.'

'Yes, isn't it funny . . .? I do hope . . .'

'You mean you know, Kate. What a pity it's such a short drive, only just time to tell you that you look very lovely; I feel very proud of you, my dear.'

She pinkened charmingly. 'The flowers are beautiful. Thank you.'

And there was no time for more. They had reached the house and there was Mary, who had rushed back from the Abbey ahead of them, waiting by the open door.

The sitting room looked delightful, crammed with flowers, its slightly shabby appearance making for comfort. They paused inside the door, and Katrina said quickly: 'Everyone's to come here first—drinks and gossip, you know, and then the food.'

'Thank God! I couldn't eat my breakfast.'

'Why ever not? It's the bride who's nervous.'

'Well, here's a bridegroom who didn't conform—I imagined you not turning up.'

'Raf—Raf, you're joking! I wouldn't do a thing like that, ever.'

He picked up her hand and kissed it. 'I know that. Before everyone comes, I've a wedding present for you.'

The box he produced was long and slender and velvet-covered; it looked old too. Inside was a pearl necklace with a diamond and sapphire clasp.

'Raf!' Katrina let out a great sigh of delight. 'It's beautiful—they're real ...' she added in something like awe.

'Yes, and very old. They're handed down to the family brides, not to be put away in a safe, but to be worn. There's a rather nice little story attached to them, I'll tell you one day.'

'Please, and thank you, Raf.' She leant up and kissed his cheek just as the first of the wedding guests came through the door.

The best man was a Dutchman, an old friend of Raf's, he assured Katrina gravely, married to one of the three women who had been at the wedding. The youngest and prettiest, too, as well as tall and well built.

'Jake and Britannia,' Raf had introduced them. 'I've known Jake for a long long time.'

He looked nice, thought Katrina, with grizzled hair and bright blue eyes which never left his wife's face for long, and she, offering a hand, confided: 'I did hope you wouldn't mind—all of us coming uninvited, you know. But Jake did promise to be best man if ever Raf married, and we do like to do everything together—so we packed up the babies and Nanny and came with him.'

Katrina beamed at her, liking her instantly. 'Of course I don't mind—I think it's lovely. But where are they—the babies?

'At my mother's—near Wareham. Twins, you know. You must come and see them, we don't live far away from Raf. I say, I do love your hat, it's quite stunning—you're just right for Raf.'

'Thank, you, Britannia,' smiled Katrina. 'Who are the other ladies?'

'Partners' wives—I expect you forgot. Raf has got two—partners, that is. They're nice. How do you like being a baroness?'

'Me?' Katrina looked astonished and then added lamely: 'Oh, I quite forgot—I always think of Raf as a professor.'

Britannia blinked. 'Well, I don't suppose you do all the time. I'm one too,' she grinned, and added disarmingly: 'I was Miss Smith.'

Katrina watched her join the others at the end of the room and felt suddenly quite lighthearted at the idea of having a new friend ready and waiting when she got to Holland. 'I like your best man and his wife,' she told Raf quietly, and held out a hand to his partners and their wives, prepared to like them too.

And less than two hours after that, she found herself sitting beside Raf in the Bentley, waving goodbye to the little group of people at the gate. Everything had happened much too quickly; she had cut the cake, but she couldn't remember eating anything, although she had had at least two glasses of champagne before going upstairs to change into the pale green knitted dress and jacket she had most extravagantly bought. She had consoled herself at the time that as she wouldn't be wearing a hat, she could afford it, and the kid sandals which went with it so well. Now, their well-wishers out of sight, she sat back for a moment, her eyes closed, and repeated her thoughts aloud.

'Everything happened much too quickly—it's like a dream.'

'Quite a nice one, I thought,' observed Raf easily, 'even though it was reality. You made a charming bride, Kate.'

They discussed their wedding at some length as they travelled north, stopping for tea presently and reaching the hotel where they were to stay the night in good time for dinner.

They were well on their way now, in Cumbria, having travelled over three hundred miles, but the Bentley had made light of it and for the

greater part of the time Raf had kept to the
motorway, but now they were in charming
country, with Bassenthwaite Lake on one side of
them and Thornwaite Forest on the other, and the
old coaching inn showing welcoming lights as they
stopped before its door.

Katrina got out of the car and looked around
her. 'Raf, however did you discover this place?
It's out of this world!'

'I stayed here once, years ago. I hope it hasn't
changed.'

They went inside and presently, her face and
hair carefully done, Katrina joined Raf in the bar.
It was still early enough in the season for the
hotel to be only half full, but that, for Katrina,
didn't matter at all; they ate their dinner at a
table in a window, with a log fire smouldering in
the hearth, and soft candlelight in place of lamps.
And afterwards they had their coffee in the drawing room, sitting in easy chairs with the table between them, talking about whatever came into
their heads. Katrina, nicely tired by now and
made even more so by the champagne she had
drunk, found her lids drooping and was thankful
when Raf said, half laughing: 'Bed for you, my
girl, before you're out cold.'

He pulled her to her feet, dropped a light kiss
on her cheek and wished her goodnight. 'Breakfast at eight?' he wanted to know. 'Or is that too
early?'

'Not a bit, but I'll have to be called.'

'I'll arrange that. Off you go.'

So she went upstairs to the delightful room on
the first floor, made short work of undressing and

bathing, and tumbled into bed. Just before she went to sleep she heard Raf's footsteps pass her door.

She was called just after seven o'clock and skipped out of bed to look out on to the lake and the mountains while she drank her tea. It was going to be a lovely day, too. She switched on the radio and whistled an accompaniment while she dressed.

Raf was already downstairs when she went to investigate, sitting outside in the sunshine, reading the newspaper, but he got up with a smile as she joined him, wished her good morning and expressed the hope that she had slept.

'Like a top. It was quite a long day, wasn't it?' She perched beside him. 'This is very nice.'

'I think so too. A pity we can't stay for a few days, but we'll come back some time if you like. I thought we'd take the Moffat road from Carlisle, we can pick up the 701 there and stop for lunch at Cringletie House just north of Peebles, there's a good restaurant there. We can go on at our leisure and get to Edinburgh in the late afternoon.'

'Are we staying near the hospital?'

'In Princes Street, at the Caledonian—not small and quiet as the Pheasant Inn was, I'm afraid, but there are conference rooms there, which makes it convenient for the various meetings, and so on. I'm afraid I shall be busy most of the time, Kate, but there's a good deal to see and some splendid shops.'

'Oh, don't worry about me, I'll do fine,' she assured him, and thought uneasily of the not very large sum of money in her purse. It seemed strange, now that she came to think about it, but they had never discussed money. Beyond assuring her that he had enough to live on in comfort, Raf had told her nothing.

But he must have read her thoughts. 'There are a great many things to discuss still, aren't there?' He glanced at her and smiled. 'If we had had a longer engagement we could have settled everything then, as it is we shall have to talk things over as we go along. You'll have an allowance, Katrina. For convenience you can draw on the account I've opened for you at my bank here. When we get home, you will have an account at my Dutch bank. Nothing to do with housekeeping . . .'

'I've a little money of my own,' she began.

'You're my wife now, Katrina, it will be my pleasure to provide for you.'

'Oh, well, thank you. I'm not extravagant.'

He didn't answer, only smiled slowly. 'Let's have breakfast.'

They had time enough to reach Edinburgh and Raf didn't hurry through the Lakes, keeping to the smaller roads until they had gone through Carlisle, but once through that city he speeded up, only slowing again to allow Katrina to look at the famous forge at Gretna Green. But they stopped at Beattock for coffee before taking the Tweedsmuir road and then making their way along country roads to Peebles.

'Heavens,' observed Katrina, seeing a signpost, 'we're not far from Edinburgh!'

'Twenty minutes, but we are going to have lunch first.'

He turned the car off the road and into a winding drive, pleasantly wooded on either side, and presently reached his goal, Cringletie House, a turreted mansion of some charm.

As Katrina got out she stared round her appreciatively. 'I say, Raf, you do know a lot of delightful places!'

He took her arm and they strolled towards the house. 'I was told of this place when I was up here last year and dined here with friends.'

What friends? Kate's mind wanted to know, but she didn't like to ask. He must have any number of friends, and some of them women. She sighed unknowingly and he said: 'Tired after all the scenery? We won't hurry over our lunch.'

And they didn't indeed; it was getting on for three o'clock before they were back on the main road once again, heading for Edinburgh.

They entered the city from the south, through the Lothian Road and so into Princes Street. The hotel was on a corner, with Arthur's Seat easily to be seen high on the hill, and below it, in Victorian grandeur, was the imposing pile of the Royal Infirmary.

'Gosh, we're right in the middle, aren't we?' said Katrina. 'Just look at the castle, did you ever see anything so absolutely splendid?'

'Magnificent, isn't it? I hope we'll have the chance to see everything. There's the Palace of Holyroodhouse too, you'll know more about that than I.'

'But I don't. Oh, I shall enjoy being here.' She turned a beaming face to him as they went into the hotel.

They had rooms on the first floor and Katrina, prowling round hers, decided that it was the height of luxury. She unpacked slowly and when Raf tapped on the door, wanted to know if she should unpack for him too. 'And what lovely rooms,' she went on happily. 'It's an enormous hotel, isn't it—I've never much fancied staying in such a vast place, but I see I was mistaken.'

Raf had gone to look out of the window. 'You prefer small hotels?' he asked carelessly.

'Yes, I think so—and the country.' She hastened to add, in case he thought that she was complaining, 'But it's nice getting the chance to explore. When do you have your lectures?'

'Nine in the morning and then again after lunch, two o'clock until half past four.' He turned to look at her. 'Oh, and on two evenings in the week there will be a conference here in this hotel. I'm afraid you won't be able to come.'

'If I see half the sights I'm sure there are to see, I'll be too tired to want to do anything in the evening.' She saw the quick frown on his face. 'Not with you, of course.'

They had tea then and went for a stroll along Princes Street and Katrina spent a blissful hour peering at the shop windows. She would certainly do some shopping, she told herself happily.

But she found that, even with so many tempting shops and visits to almost every museum in the city, she was lonely. She saw Raf briefly at breakfast and then again at lunch, but then he was preoccupied with the afternoon's work ahead of him so that conversation, although easy enough, was at a minimum. But he always enquired after her morning and listened apparently with interest to her carefully pruned accounts of the places she had visited. She took care not to chat, though, and was rewarded after a few days by his: 'I can see that I have married a treasure— not so much as a tiny moan from you, and I've left you alone for several days now.'

'We have our evenings,' she pointed out.

He smiled at her. 'Indeed we have, and very nice they are, too.'

Katrina agreed with him silently; they dined and danced each evening, sometimes at the hotel but once or twice at hotels a little way from the city's heart—Prestonfield House, which she liked very much, and the Inn at Cramond, where they dined in an oak-beamed room, close to the harbour.

It was on their last day in Edinburgh that she asked him, a little diffidently, if she might attend his lecture.

Raf looked taken aback. 'My dear girl, whatever for? You'll be bored to tears in half an hour. You'll enjoy yourself far more doing some last-minute shopping.'

She had agreed with him quietly and then gone out and spent a good deal of money in a reckless fashion on shoes which she didn't really want and a silk trouser suit which she was sure she would never wear. And when Raf asked her at lunch time what she had done with herself, she told him, not mincing her words.

'You told me to go shopping, so I did. I bought some wildly expensive shoes that don't go with anything I've got, and I bought a trouser suit—

blue silk with flowers all over it. I can't think when I shall ever wear it.'

'Why, at home in the evenings, I hope, to cheer me up when I come home tired.' He was smiling a little and it annoyed her.

'I didn't think of that,' she told him. 'I bought it because I just wanted to waste your money; it would have cost you far less to have let me come to the lecture.'

His eyebrows shot up. 'Ah, here we have it. Am I to understand that each time I—er—decline your company you will rush to the nearest shop and buy unsuitable clothes out of revenge?'

'Yes, if you like to put it that way—and I daresay,' added Katrina with some heat, 'my wardrobe will be bulging in no time at all!'

He spoke smoothly. 'Are we having our first quarrel, Katrina?'

She looked at him bewildered. 'No—no, of course not. I snapped, and I'm sorry. It's just that I want to know more about you.' She didn't see the sudden gleam in his eyes. When he spoke his voice was kind and understanding.

'Then you will attend one of my lectures in Holland—that's a promise.' He hesitated. 'I'm sorry, but there's a final short meeting this evening—here at the hotel. Will you be all right on your own? It's at eight o'clock and should last no more than an hour.'

Katrina had promised herself that she would make him a good wife. She said brightly: 'Of course. Shall we dine early or would you rather wait until it's over.'

'Oh, before I think, don't you?' He glanced at

his watch. 'I must be off—I should be back around four o'clock. We might stroll round the shops.'

'That would be nice.' She smiled him a cheerful goodbye.

They had tea out, at a dear little teashop, all chintz and flowered china, a fitting background for the paper-thin sandwiches and cakes oozing cream.

'I ought not to,' said Katrina, having a second one.

Raf eyed her across the little table. 'Why not? You don't have to starve yourself on my account. I like curves.'

She went a delicate pink. 'Yes, well ...' she began uncertainly. 'It's bad enough being so big, I don't want to get fat.'

'You won't. Besides, we shall walk miles during the next few days, you'll need all your strength.'

They wandered down Princes Street, pausing to look at everything which caught their eye, and when Katrina remarked on a handbag, displayed in unpriced state on a length of velvet, Raf walked her into the shop and bought it for her, and when she thanked him and protested at his extravagance he remarked easily: 'Ah, but it's an investment—it will last you a lifetime.'

She brightened. 'So it will—I'll take great care of it, Raf.'

They left Edinburgh early the next morning, taking the motorway to Stirling and then on to Callender and so to Lochearnhead, where they stopped for lunch. They were in the Highlands now, and Katrina was loving every moment of it. 'I could go on for ever like this,' she told Raf. 'There couldn't be anything more beautiful.'

'Wait until you see the Isle of Eriska,' he promised her.

They reached it, not having hurried, in the late afternoon, crossing the small bridge from the mainland and following the track, bordered by shrubs and conifers, to the hotel.

It didn't look in the least like a hotel; it had battlements and turrets and gabled windows and inside it was warmly welcoming with tea in the library, where a log fire burned cheerfully and the proprietor joined them briefly, chatting about Raf's last visit, recommending some walks they might like to take and then handing them over to a pleasant girl who took them to their rooms and offered to unpack for them—an offer Katrina declined, happily putting her things away and then going through to Raf's room to see if she could do the same for him.

They dined off fresh salmon, a magnificent salad and apricot brulée, and joined the other guests for coffee in the library, and presently tired with her exciting day, Katrina said goodnight and went upstairs. Raf had gone to the door with her and stood a moment holding it open.

'We might try one of those walks tomorrow,' he suggested. 'I'm told the weather is going to be good for a few days at least.'

'Lovely. It's beautiful here, Raf—what a marvellous holiday!'

His mouth twitched faintly as he wished her goodnight.

They had five days there, and every one better than the last, thought Katrina on their last evening. They had walked, picnicked and fished, sat in the sun and read and talked unendingly. At last she felt that she was beginning to know Raf, although there was a great deal more she still had to discover. That they were happy in each other's company was a solid fact upon which she felt they would build a happy marriage, and they were friends, too, and if once or twice she found herself wishing that Raf behaved rather more like a husband and less like a lifelong friend, she didn't allow herself to brood over it. After all, he had to get to know her too.

They left quite early in the morning, the Bentley making light work of the run down to Carlisle and then on to Crooklands where they spent the night; a country inn in Cumbria, peaceful and quiet but near enough to the M6 to make it a matter of minutes before they joined it.

It was a long trip to London and Raf kept to the motorway, leaving it for a short time south of Stoke-on-Trent so that they might have coffee and then again, once they were through Birmingham, for lunch at a village inn before getting on to the M1.

'Tired?' he wanted to know, as he started the car. 'It's only just over a hundred miles now.'

Katrina wasn't tired, the Bentley was too comfortable and Raf drove superbly, so that she was completely relaxed. 'You didn't say where we're spending the night,' she observed. 'In London?'

'Yes, at my flat.'

She turned to look at him. 'Your flat? Have

you got one there?'

'Well, I come over to England quite a lot, you know.'

'No, I didn't', said Katrina a shade tartly. 'I supposed you stayed with Uncle Ben.'

'It quite slipped my mind.' Raf sounded so meek that she looked at him again, but he was staring ahead, his profile as calm as always. 'It's only small, but I have a good housekeeper. She'll have a meal ready for us.'

She longed to ask more questions, but although she was his wife she didn't want to be nosey, and after all, they would be there within an hour or so and she would see for herself.

It took some time to penetrate London: the rush hour was just starting and it was a little while before she saw that Raf was working his way towards Hyde Park Corner and then turned north of Piccadilly into one of the quiet streets there, to stop at last before a town house of some size with an important porch and flower boxes at the windows.

Inside it was cool and very quiet, with a door on either side of the wide hall, but Raf ignored them and went up the staircase between them, taking her with him. On the landing he took out a key and opened one of the doors and ushered her inside, and she realised at once that his idea of small was hardly hers. The hall was narrow, it was true, thickly carpeted and pleasantly lighted; it led to a sitting-room of a size and height which she described to herself as vast, although charmingly furnished, but before she could say a word an elderly woman joined them to be greeted by the professor with: 'Ah, Mrs Thomas, Katrina, my dear, this is Mrs Thomas, our housekeeper. I expect you'd like to see your room first, wouldn't you? There'll be time for a drink before dinner.'

Katrina went with Mrs Thomas, still not having uttered a word, feeling at a disadvantage. He could have told her about the flat; they'd been married almost two weeks and heaven knew they'd had plenty of time to talk. She tidied herself in the charming room she had been taken to and hurried back to the sitting-room.

'You could have told me,' she said crossly, and when he asked mildly: 'Told you what my dear?' snapped: 'About this flat, of course.'

He said casually: 'It didn't seem important to me—to you, either.'

'Yes, but don't you see? It's—it's like having secrets . . .'

He came across the room and took her hands in his. 'Kate, if I have any secrets from you, they're harmless ones. After all, if we had had a long engagement, you wouldn't have discovered all there was to know about me in a couple of weeks, would you?'

She saw that this was a reasonable remark. 'Well, no. I'm sorry if I made a fuss.'

He gave her back her hands and walked away from her to a sofa table holding a tray of drinks. 'And now what will you drink?'

So they weren't to talk about it any more, she thought; perhaps it was early days for them to be quite—she was at a loss for a word.

The dinner was excellent, served in a much smaller room, elegantly furnished, and after an hour's gentle conversation, mostly on the part of Raf, Katrina went to bed. Her teeth clenched on the numerous questions she was dying to ask. Was the flat rented? she wondered, and did Mrs Thomas live there all the time? Wasn't that rather extravagant when Raf only came to London every so often? She thought uneasily of the Bentley and his handmade shoes and silk shirts and beautifully tailored clothes—perhaps he was rich, not just comfortably off but really rich, in which case why couldn't he have said so? Or was he waiting for her to ask him outright? Sleepy though she was, she began trying out various ways of putting the question. Should she baldly ask: 'Are you rich, Raf?' or put it more politely: 'I suppose you've got a lot of money?' or even try a round-about way: 'Are you sure you can afford to run a Bentley?' None of them sounded right; she gave up and went to sleep.

CHAPTER SIX

Raf had an appointment at Benedict's in the morning and it had been arranged that he should drive Katrina to Aunt Lucy's house and join her there for lunch, bringing Uncle Ben with him. Katrina, left on her own with Aunt Lucy, drank coffee, answered a great many questions and gave a detailed account of their stay in Scotland.

'A pity you haven't been able to see your dear mother,' commented her companion, 'but of course, Raf is a busy man. Did you like his partners, dear?'

Katrina said that she did, their wives too, 'And his best man—I thought his wife was a dear—I hope we'll see something of each other in Holland.'

Aunt Lucy murmured comfortably and went on to discuss the wedding at some length. She was still explaining, rather vaguely, why she had chosen a grey outfit for the occasion when the men came in and Katrina found herself with Uncle Ben, listening to his pithy account of his morning rounds. 'There was this terrible Staff Nurse—Adams, I think she's called, queening it round the place—she didn't seem very popular. It needs you there to get them into line, Kate . . .'

'Over my dead body,' observed Raf without heat, and Uncle Ben laughed and added:

'I keep forgetting that you two are married.'

He looked at Katrina. 'You enjoyed Scotland, Raf tells me.'

Katrina plunged into her second time round account of their holiday, and it lasted nicely through drinks and the first part of lunch. The second part was largely taken up with a discussion between the two men as to the exact date of a seminar they both wished to attend.

'Well, if it's to be in Birmingham,' said Uncle Ben, finally, 'you can bring Kate over with you.' He beamed at them both. 'You're going on the Harwich night boat, I suppose?'

They went back to the flat later, and Katrina busied herself repacking her case with the things the housekeeper had washed and pressed for her. She had another case too, of clothes she hadn't needed to take to Scotland; she disposed of those in her neat fashion, and enquired of Raf if she should do the same for him, but it seemed that Mrs Thomas had already done that, so there was nothing more for her to do but sit quietly. Raf had gone to his study down the hall, saying in the nicest possible way that he didn't want to be disturbed; she leafed through a pile of magazines and tried not to get agitated at the thought of going to a new house in another country. Supposing she hated it, supposing they found they couldn't get on together, supposing ... She called a halt; she was a grown woman, used to dealing with emergencies, difficult people, running a ward successfully and surely not so poorspirited that she couldn't make a success of their marriage. After all, she had gone into it with her eyes open and with a mind clear of infatuation.

She reviewed the number of her friends and acquaintances who had married for love on the spur of the moment and come a cropper. Well, she had married on the spur of the moment, too, but in full possession of her senses, thank heaven, and as for Raf, she couldn't imagine him anything but placid; even when he was annoying her, he was calm about it.

They left London in the early evening, dined on the way to Harwich and went on board just before the ferry was due to sail. Katrina, inspecting her cabin, was impressed by its comfort although she wasn't sure if she was going to sleep soundly, but a brisk walk round the deck with Raf and a drink in the bar made her change her mind; besides, she had to be up early in the morning and look her best. She got into her narrow bed and closed her eyes determinedly and was asleep within minutes.

In the early morning light, the Hoek van Holland looked very like Harwich, only the people around her were speaking another language, even Raf, who switched from one language to the other without effort.

Sitting beside him in the Bentley, she was suddenly shaken by doubts again, and turned a bewildered face to his, to be instantly reassured by his understanding smile and a firm hand on her own two, lying tense in her lap.

'We'll soon be home, my dear,' he said placidly, and everything was normal once more.

He took the road to Den Haag, turning away from that city on its southern outskirts and taking a lesser road to join the motorway to Leiden, but before they reached the first of its houses, Raf turned away from the road again on to a narrow sandy road which led them within minutes to a small village. After the rush of traffic on the motorway barely a mile away, the rural quiet was pleasant and when Raf slowed and stopped outside the village café and she looked questioningly at him, he said: 'I thought a cup of coffee . . . no tea, I'm afraid, but the coffee's good.'

The narrow street was empty of people, it was still so early and there was nothing to break the stillness except the birds. 'Oh, a cuckoo!' exclaimed Katrina. 'It's . . .'

'And after April, when May follows,' interrupted Raf. 'That's almost the first thing we said to each other.'

'Yes—I didn't think . . . that is, I would never have guessed that by May we would be married, would you?'

He didn't answer her, but she didn't notice because a jolly old man had opened the café door and called something.

'He's telling us that the coffee is ready and waiting,' said Raf, and ushered her inside.

They went back on to the motorway presently, allowing Katrina only a glimpse of Leiden on their left, but as they reached the last houses of the small city Raf left the motorway for a minor road and this in its turn became a narrow country lane. 'We're almost there,' he told her. 'If you look to your left you'll see Warmond and in the other direction is Rijpwetering, large villages both of them. The water ahead of us is the Kager Plassen, there's a good deal of sailing in the summer and if it freezes hard enough, skating in the winter.'

Katrina stared round her. The country was flat and gentle; water meadows with cattle standing quietly. They were on a dyke road now, with a narrow canal on either side and a mile ahead she could see the lake quite clearly, ringed with shrubs and clusters of trees. 'It's nice,' she said. 'Do you know, I've not thought much about your home—you said it was in the country, but I hadn't pictured it in my mind. Is there a village?'

'In the trees close to the lake—a very small one, but there's a shop and a church and a school for the small children—the others go to Warmond.'

'You live in the village?'

She wondered why he hesitated. 'On the fringe.'

The village came into view a moment later, a cluster of neat cottages with a church, much too large for them, in the centre of an open grassed square. There were several people about now, and they smiled and nodded at Raf, who lifted a hand in greeting as he slowed the car round the church. Katrina, looking about her, tried to decide which house was his. There were two or three villas in between the cottages, but none of them really looked like a doctor's house; besides, he had said he lived on the edge of the village. The road straightened out on the other side of the square with tall trees on either side of it and thick shrubs behind which she glimpsed high old-fashioned iron railings. And round the bend there were high wrought iron gates, opening on to a sanded drive and at the end of it, a house.

'This isn't . . .' began Katrina, eyeing its solid white plastered walls and high shuttered windows with utter surprise. 'It can't be . . .'

'Yes, it is.'

She looked again; it wasn't of great architectural beauty, perhaps, but it looked just right, standing as it did with trees in a semicircle behind it and a formal garden in front. Its steep roof was grey-slated and every window gleamed in the morning sun. She counted them; there were twenty of them, and up in the roof there were small shuttered windows, the shutters painted red and white and green, each of them crowned with a kind of tiled frill. 'You should have told me,' she muttered.

'Are you disappointed, Kate?'

'Disappointed? Of course not!' Her voice rose a little. 'It's beautiful, but it's so enormous—I didn't know—I'll make a mess of it, being your wife and living in a place like this,' she added, quite worked up by now, 'and I suppose you're stinking rich as well!'

Raf stopped the car and turned to look at her. 'Now you see why I didn't tell you, my dear. You would have shied away like a startled pony, gone to the Gulf and probably become a dedicated spinster. There is no possible reason for you to worry about making—er—a mess of living here, you will be welcomed and liked by everyone.' He sounded matter-of-fact and a little amused. 'And I am stinking rich!'

'Oh,' said Katrina, 'I'm sorry, I shouldn't have said that—it's none of my business . . .'

He gave a crack of laughter. 'It is, you know—

you'll have to learn all the business of the estate so that if I'm away for any reason, you can carry on.'

'But it's all Dutch!' She was horrified.

'You'll learn very quickly—Caspel speaks a little English, so does the *dominee* in the village and the schoolteacher. And Nanny, of course.'

'You make it sound so easy!'

'And you, my dear, are making a great fuss about nothing.' He spoke pleasantly, but she blushed scarlet.

'I'll not make a fuss again, I promise you,' she told him in a wooden voice.

She would have liked to burst into tears, boxed his ears and then been soothed to calmness again; as it was she took a deep breath and remarked in an over-bright voice: 'How very pretty it is—I expect the garden runs down to the lake on that side?'

'Yes, there is a boat-house there and a small landing stage.' Nothing in his voice gave her a clue as to what he was thinking. He was going to be impossible to quarrel with, she thought pettishly, and then pulled herself up sharply. This was no way in which to begin life in her new home; she would do everything to conform to Raf's idea of a good wife. And the first thing was to accept everything without question, learn the language, and learn to run his home as he wanted it.

He started the car again and drove the last hundred yards or so to where Caspel was standing by the open door.

And not just Caspel. As she walked up the

steps beside Raf, Katrina saw several other
people standing beside him. Raf greeted them
and then introduced her; Caspel, his wife Berthe,
Wibrich and Jildou, the two young maids, Franz
the gardener, and someone called Mevrouw Boot,
whose position in the household was rather
vague. Nanny was in her room and after a welcoming speech from Caspel on behalf of the others,
and which she couldn't understand anyway, Katrina was taken to see her.

The hall they were standing in was large and
square, with heavy side tables and several large
chairs. There were portraits on its white walls
and an enormous chandelier overhead. Katrina
would have liked time to examine it, but Raf had
a hand on her arm, leading her down a short passage at the back of the hall, to the side of the
curving staircase.

Nanny, being old, lived on the ground floor.
'She suffers from arthritis,' explained Raf, 'but
hates to be shut away, and here she gets visited
by anyone who happens to be passing.'

He knocked on a door at the end of the passage
and went in, taking Katrina with him.

The room was a surprise, it was so very English, with cretonne covers on the chairs, and
matching curtains at the window, a table in the
centre with an old-fashioned serge cloth on it and
a great many shelves and little tables, all
crammed with photos and china ornaments—the
kind of ornaments friends are prone to give when
they've been on holiday. And in the middle of
this sat Nanny, small and bony and bent. But she
had a sweet face and bright blue eyes, as guileless

as a child's.

Raf hugged her gently and kissed her. 'Well, Nanny, here she is—my wife, Katrina,' he had gone back to take her hand, 'I hope that you and Nanny will be friends, just as she and I have been friends.'

Katrina put out a hand. 'May I call you Nanny?' she asked. 'I'm so glad you're here, I don't know anything about Holland and I'll be so happy to have your help and advice.'

Nanny pushed her glasses up her nose. 'Freely given, Baroness. You just come along and talk to Nanny whenever you want to. You're a bonny girl, too—just right for Master Raf. We'll have a nice little chat one day soon.'

Outside the door, Katrina said: 'What a darling old lady, and she looks so happy and content—those poor hands, all knotted up.'

'Not so old either—seventy-three, but she's suffered a good deal. She was away from my home when they came for my parents, and when she found out what had happened and that the Caspels were already on the way to my grandparents, she decided to follow. Only she was caught on the way—she would have been sent to a prison-camp, but it just so happened that some official or other was taken ill and she knew what to do for him. They let her stay alive then, working in the hospital half starved and sleeping in a damp cellar. I can just remember the fuss I made because she had disappeared from my world too. Once the war was over my grandfather set about finding her; it took a long time.'

'And has she been with you ever since?'

'Of course, and will stay.'

He looked a little grim, so she didn't say any more, only agreed pleasantly when he suggested that she might like to see her room.

Berthe took her upstairs, moving slowly because she was on the stout side, which gave Katrina time to look around her. The stairs swept up one side of the hall to curve into a gallery above. They walked along one side of it to the front of the house and Berthe opened a pair of doors in the centre of the wide corridor. The room was quite beautiful, with a high ceiling covered with intricate plaster work and deeply carpeted in a thick cream pile. The bed had a mahogany headboard inlaid with a marquetry of flowers and fruit in woods of all colours; its spread of cream silk had a pattern of blue birds and pale pink roses and was quilted, matching the curtains at the high, wide windows. There was a sofa table in one corner with a triple mirror on it and a tallboy, its bowed front covered with the same marquetry as on the bed. The chairs were covered in a pale blue velvet and the walls were hung with striped cream silk with groups of small flower paintings hung here and there, the whole lighted by rose-tinted lamps.

Katrina drew a long breath. It was the loveliest room she had ever seen, and it seemed that it was to be hers.

Berthe, watching her, smiled and nodded and crossed the room to open a door in the opposite wall; a bathroom, blue and white, with a thickly carpeted floor and glass shelves stacked with blue and white towels. There would be blue soap, thought Katrina, and went to look. There was.

There was no sign of her luggage; she would unpack later. She smiled dismissal of Berthe and went to sit before the mirror, noticing for the first time that the table was gleaming with silver—brushes and comb, mirror and small silver and cut glass bowls. She picked up the brush, plain silver, initialled in the centre. Her eyes widened. Coincidence, of course, but the initials were hers.

She tidied her hair, did things to her face, and went downstairs to find Raf waiting for her in the hall.

'The luggage will be taken up while we lunch,' he told her, 'and someone will unpack for you. I hope you like your room?'

'It's beautiful,' she assured him, 'quite the most beautiful I've ever seen.'

He turned away. 'The things on the dressing table are a wedding present, the pearls have been in the family for a long time. I wanted to give you something I had chosen myself.'

She hurried across the tiled floor. 'Raf, they're absolutely lovely—thank you very much. When I saw then I wondered . . .' she smiled rather shyly. 'I thought perhaps they were your mother's and by some coincidence we had the same initials.'

'She had a Friese name, Jikkemien; she was christened Jacomina, but it was quickly changed to the Friese form.'

'And very pretty it sounds, although I like Jacomina, too. Was your father called Raf?'

'Yes, and his father before him—a Dutch custom, fast dying out.' He smiled at her. 'There would be old Raf and young Raf; very confusing.'

'But nice to keep the name in the family.' She looked up and saw his eyes upon her and looked away quickly; probably he thought that she was being a bit sloppy and sentimental. 'I heard a dog barking while I was upstairs,' she observed brightly

He seemed content to change the conversation. 'That is Boots—a black labrador. I have another dog, too—a Corgi called Vondel.'

'But I thought he was a Dutch poet . . .'

'So he was—I found Vondel in Vondel Park, tied to a tree: he was a very small puppy.'

'Oh, how beastly; I'm glad you found him— and Boots? Don't tell me you found him too?'

Raf laughed. 'Well, yes—lying in the doorway of a chemist's shop in Den Haag.' He took her arm. 'Come and meet them.'

After the initial surprise it seemed to Katrina that she had lived all her life in Huis Tellerinck. For one thing she was accepted at once, smoothly integrated into the house, helped enormously by Caspel and Berthe, who unobtrusively showed her the routine of the household, indicated which tasks she might be expected to do; the flowers, the morning visit to the roomy kitchen, the inspecting of the linen cupboards, and what was most important, Raf's likes and dislikes. He wasn't a fussy man, she discovered, but he liked things just so and the house was geared so that when he returned home in the evening or late afternoon, it welcomed him with its gleaming furniture, its bowls of flowers and its air of peace.

And Katrina welcomed him too, surprised to find herself looking forward to his return each day, taking trouble with her hair and face and putting on a pretty dress, learning within a few days to read his face as he came in and being careful to adjust her own mood to his. It was on the fourth evening after they were back that she asked him a little diffidently if he never came home for lunch. She had been occupied with some needlework and hadn't given him more than a quick glance, so that she missed the long thoughtful look he gave her and his slow smile.

'Would you like me to come home during the day?' he asked her.

Katrina bit off her thread. 'Oh, yes—I'm not lonely, you know, but it would be nice to hear how your day's going, only I can quite see that you might not want to; it must be convenient to lunch in hospital or—or wherever you are.'

His smile widened. 'Where else might I be, Kate?'

She was untangling a skein of silk. 'Well, I don't know that, do I? Friends—perhaps . . .' A vivid picture of him lunching with some beautiful girl-friend from his bachelor days made her scowl.

'I always found it a little lonely lunching alone at home,' he said placidly, 'and I thought that you might prefer to have the day to yourself . . .'

'Raf, whatever made you think that? I'd love you to come to lunch at home, only I thought, when you stayed away the first day, that it was what you always did and I didn't want to interfere . . .'

'I can't imagine that you would do that.' His calm voice soothed her ruffled feelings. 'I said before we married, Kate, that we would have to get to know each other.'

'Yes, I know.' She wanted to add that there was a great deal she would like to know about him: his friends, if he had ever been engaged or been in love ... he must have been. She wondered where the girl was now—perhaps more than one girl. She pricked her finger and sucked it; it would be nice when they were sufficiently old friends to be able to ask these things. She didn't quite have the courage to question him now; he would treat her to a bland look and one of those smiles which meant that he was amused at her.

She said into the small silence: 'So you'll come for lunch when you can?'

'Certainly—I should manage to get home about half past twelve; if I can't I'll telephone.'

She wasn't sure what made her ask: 'And breakfast? I expect you like to be alone then?'

'I've had my breakfast alone for a number of years, Katrina,' he reminded her, 'and rather early—half past seven most mornings, but if you don't mind getting up early, I should enjoy your company very much. I can't guarantee to have much conversation, though.'

She felt out of all proportion delighted. 'Oh, I'll not say a word unless you actually speak,' she promised him.

And it worked very well; it was surprising what a difference it made to her days too, even though Raf, for the most part, sat frowning over papers or his post while he ate his breakfast she didn't mind, for every so often he would look up and smile and once or twice he remarked on something she was wearing. But lunchtime was even better; she took care to have a drink waiting for him and lunch ready to be served, carefully thought out food which he could eat quickly if he had an early appointment after lunch. At the end of ten days, Katrina had found her feet. She had inspected the house from cellar to attics and loved every inch of it, she had wrestled with menus and grocery lists under the kindly eye of Berthe, she had even picked up a few useful words in Dutch, although it still sounded nonsense in her ears.

She hadn't done badly, she considered, sitting in the drawing-room waiting for Raf to come home from his day's work. She had put on one of her new dresses, a pale green crepe very simply made and she knew she looked nice, sitting there, her embroidery in her hand, the evening sun lighting up the charming room with its beautiful furnishings. She hoped she was proving to be the kind of wife Raf had wanted. There was a lot to learn still, of course, and the rather frightening prospect of meeting his friends—if they were half as nice as Britannia and Jake then everything would be all right.

An invitation had come that very morning from Britannia, asking them to go over to dinner in four days' time; she would show it to Raf when he got in. He agreed at once, but she hadn't expected otherwise. Moreover, he suggested that since he was free for the weekend, they should go to the sea the next day. 'You've not had much fun, have you?' he observed, 'and I've had my nose to the grindstone and my hand on the scalpel ... we'll go to Katwijk-aan-Zee, early in the morning, and drive up the coast. At least, we'll park the car just outside the town and walk along the dunes and take the road again when we're tired. Would you like that?'

'Oh, yes—lovely.' A whole day with him, a day in which to learn a lot more about him, his work, for instance, and his life before they married, and his friends ... especially did she want to know about them. She wasn't jealous, she told herself as she got ready for bed, that would be absurd, only curious. She would wear the blue and white striped separates, then if it got really warm she could leave the jacket in the car ... and her new sandals, the ones with the low heels.

They left the house really early after breakfast and they were there, standing on the wide golden sands within half an hour. There was no one around, the sea stretched away to the horizon, a choppy sea, whipped up by the sharp wind which was freshening at every minute. It took Katrina's hair and tossed it round her shoulders, and when she would have stopped and tied it back, Raf said, 'No, leave it,' and flung an arm round her shoulders as they walked. He was relaxed, placid almost to the point of sleepiness, and in his linen slacks and cotton sweater, he looked younger. They didn't bother to talk a great deal, odds and ends of gossip, arrangements for going to Britannia's home during the week, tentative suggestions for a small dinner party, the possibility of Katrina visiting the hospital in Leiden. They were discussing this when Raf paused and then stopped dead.

'There's a yacht . . .' he said thoughtfully. 'I noticed it just now—whoever is sailing it is a fool, the red flag's out and he must have seen it—there's quite a current along here, and the wind is pretty strong.' He stared out to sea, his arm still round Katrina. 'He's coming much too far in-shore.'

As he spoke the yacht veered into the wind, racing off on a different course, only to veer again, sailing towards them again.

'Perhaps there's no one on board,' suggested Katrina, and then cried: 'Oh, but there is—there's a child crying!'

A small screaming voice could be faintly heard as the yacht drew nearer and Raf said un-hurriedly: 'I'll just take a look—no one in their senses would sail like that, and if they're in trouble why don't they shout?'

He took off his shoes and walked into the water without another word. The yacht was going out to sea again and Katrina reckoned that it was roughly a quarter of a mile away. Raf was swimming now and without further ado she took off her own sandals and went in after him; she was a strong swimmer and could do a mile in a calm sea. But this sea was decidedly choppy and before she had gone very far she encountered the current Raf had mentioned. Just for a moment she felt panicky, but the yacht was coming in-shore once more and wasn't all that way off now. She rested briefly and went on, swimming strongly. She hadn't seen Raf get on board, but he would be there by now.

She reached the yacht presently and heaved herself untidily on to its deck, streaming water and shivering a little now. The child was still screaming and she got to her feet, staggering a little with the boat's movement, and went below. There was a child all right, three years old perhaps, a boy, bawling his small head off, sitting in one of the bunks watching Raf bending over someone lying on the floor of the cabin.

'Hullo,' said Katrina, not knowing what else to say and Raf looked up.

'Ah, just the girl I wanted—concussion and a smashed leg. Find a broom handle or something, will you, and bring them here and then hang on while I get it splinted. I think I've got it in alignment.'

His voice was almost casual and he evinced no surprise at her appearance; she said nothing at all, but began her search. There was a child's wooden spade lying in one corner, and in the kitchen a handled mop; Katrina couldn't get the mop off, so she took it to Raf and offered it with the spade. 'Splendid,' he said, 'and something to tie them with.'

She took the sopping tie belt from her waist—the dress was ruined anyway—sawed it in half with a knife from the galley and handed the pieces to him.

'Very nice, my dear. Now come here and take the leg from me—you'll need to keep a good pull on it.'

She applied traction while he applied the makeshift splints. They looked peculiar when he had finished, but at least they were doing their work.

'Leave him here,' said Raf, and put a cushion gently under the unconscious head. 'I'm going up to see if I can sail this boat in, you see if you can pacify that unhappy scrap.'

He had gone, leaving her to cover the man with a blanket and then take the weeping child on her wet knee and soothe it to quietness, wondering as she did so what would have happened if she hadn't been able to swim. The boy quietened presently and quite soon worn out with fright, dropped off to sleep. Katrina tucked him up securely, took a look at the man, and took his pulse, and went on deck.

Raf was at the rudder, working the boat slowly towards the shore. 'We're going to end up at Noordwijk,' he told her cheerfully. 'Everything quiet below?'

'The little boy's asleep, the man's still unconscious—his pulse isn't too bad—just over a hundred, but it's quite steady.'

He nodded, smiling at her. 'You're wet—it suits you.' He looked away from her, towards the nearing shore.

Was this all she was to get for her pains? She had, after all, swum a considerable distance in a nasty sea, ruined a dress, produced splints when asked for them, suffered aching arms from pulling on a large and very heavy broken leg, soothed a child when she badly needed soothing herself ... he was indifferent to her, arrogant, thoughtless, overbearing. Katrina, normally a mild-tempered girl, was possessed of a splendid rage, then in a twinkling of an eye it had evaporated because at that precise moment she became aware that she was head over heels in love with Raf.

She stood, the blue and white stripes clinging wetly to her magnificent figure, quite unaware of the delightful picture she made, and gaped at him. There was an awful lot she wanted to say, but her thoughts were in such a jumble she was unable to put them into words—and anyway, she wasn't given the chance. Raf looked at her for a long moment, his eyes almost hidden beneath their lids and then he looked away again.

'We're almost in,' he said in a detached voice. 'Would you like to go below and rouse the little one?'

She didn't trust herself to speak, and as she slipped and slithered into the cabin she thanked heaven that she had held her tongue.

CHAPTER SEVEN

RAF had made for a jetty in the small harbour at the end of the little town. He tied up neatly, shouted to a man lounging over the rail watching them and went below.

Katrina had had a few minutes in which to pull herself together; she felt lightheaded, excited and at the same time ready to burst into tears; all the same, she had roused the little boy and was tidying him up as Raf joined them. He said something to the child and went to look at the man. 'I've asked someone to fetch the police and an ambulance,' he said. 'The quicker this man's in hospital the better.'

For something to say, Katrina asked: 'Is there a hospital here?'

'They'll take him to Leiden, it's the nearest, if he goes to Katwijk he'll probably be transferred. I wonder who he is?'

'The child?' She was quick to understand him.

'The police will look after him while they get his mother.' He lifted his head. 'Here they are now.'

The police car and the ambulance arrived together and it was at once apparent that the police and the ambulance men knew Raf. They listened to his brief story and then the ambulance men, under his guidance, re-splintered the injured man's leg and carried him to the ambulance while

the police carred a surprisingly docile little boy to
their car. They knew the man, they even knew
where he lived, and a message was sent out to
fetch the mother while the senior officer wrote in
his notebook.

Katrina sat on the side of the jetty, watching.
To all intents and purposes, she might not have
been there. The men had saluted her politely and
then ignored her and beyond a brief: 'O.K.,
Kate?' Raf hadn't looked at her once. A pity I'm
not a dainty mouse of a creature, prone to faint-
ing, she thought crossly as she watched her husband dealing with the situation in his calm way.
And finally, when the constable had at last put
his notebook away, Raf said something to him
which sent him to the car's radio. Only then did
Raf join her.

'They'll drive us back to Katwijk,' he told her.
'We'll have to go back home and change our
clothes.' Just for a moment he rested a hand on
her knee. 'I'm sorry, my dear, but there really
wasn't anything else to do.'

Her heart was thudding away, making such a
noise in her ears that she was afraid that he would
hear it too. 'Of course not—thank heaven you
were there to help.'

'And thank heaven you were there, Kate. I
don't know why, but I took it for granted that
you would be right beside me, and you were.'

The pink crept into her cheeks. She was going
to say something about wives helping their husbands; she might even have said more than that,
only he answered her with a prosaic: 'I expect it's
your hospital training—once a nurse, always a

nurse.'

She looked away, choking back a strong desire to burst into tears. After a moment she said in a brittle voice: 'Here's another police car coming.'

Raf was watching her; he looked thoughtful and at the same time pleased, as he said casually: 'A pity about the dress, it was charming. We'll have to get another one exactly like it.' He got to his feet and pulled her to hers. 'I'll just have a final word—jump in, my dear.'

A moment later he got in beside the driver and turned to speak to her. 'The mother's on the way. I'll telephone the hospital when we get home.'

Her lovely day was ruined. Raf would spend the rest of it in Leiden, she supposed. Well, she would get into a swimsuit and spend an hour in the swimming pool behind the house, then she would go for a good long walk and try and sort things out. There was a lot of thinking to be done. The thought uppermost in her head at the moment was that Raf must never guess that she loved him. She would have to go on just as always, good friends and companions with each other, and she learning to be a good hostess and manager of his home, and perhaps in time he would learn to love her too—just a little would do . . .

The journey was a brief one, they transferred themselves into the Bentley and drove home, not talking much. Once there, Raf explained what had happened with no fuss and in the shortest space of time and then bore Katrina off to the library where Caspel followed them with hot coffee and brandy.

'But we'll ruin the furniture,' objected Katrina. 'I'm still damp and so are you.'

But her objections were ignored; she was given coffee to drink with a stiff dose of brandy in it and then told to go and have a hot bath and put on dry clothing. 'Half an hour,' suggested Raf. 'We'll drive into Leiden and if I have to stay more than a few minutes at the hospital you shall go on a tour of inspection, but I don't expect to. We'll go back to Noordwijk for lunch, there's a rather nice hotel, Huis ter Duin, overlooking the sea. We can drive on up the coast as far as Alkmaar and come home along the inner road.'

Katrina was on her feet, starting for the door. 'Oh, that sounds heavenly!' She suddenly remembered that she must stay friendly and nothing more. 'That's if you would like to too.'

Raf had reached the door and was opening it for her. 'I can think of nothing I'd like better,' he told her. He stood looking down at her, smiling a little. 'Quite an adventure, wasn't it? It didn't upset you?'

'Me, upset? No, of course not—it all happened rather quickly, didn't it?'

'Indeed, yes—one rarely has forewarning of the more dramatic moments in life. Have you found that too?'

A bit near the bone; in another moment she would be telling him that she had had a dramatic moment when she discovered that she loved him, not two hours ago. She muttered 'Yes' as she passed him, but he put out a leisurely arm and held her for a moment, to kiss her on her surprised mouth.

She didn't allow herself to think while she bathed and dressed. There wasn't much time, anyway, for she had her hair to wash too. She had no leisure to fuss over it, leaving it, very clean and shining to swing round her shoulders. It was a pity about the blue and white striped dress, she thought as she got into a cotton voile, lemon and lime stripes on a white ground, and just in case it should turn chilly, she snatched up a white blazer before she ran downstairs.

The rest of the day was heaven. Raf spent no more than fifteen minutes at the hospital, looking at X-rays, giving instructions for his latest patient's treatment, and while he was away, Katrina was entertained by the Directrice, a rather formidable lady whose excellent command of English allowed her to ask polite but searching questions of her while she drank a cup of coffee she didn't want.

Raf, coming to fetch her, smiled very faintly at Katrina's determined but polite efforts not to answer any questions at all, and stood listening with a bland face while she thanked the Directrice and said that yes, she'd love to come again and spend an hour or two over a cup of coffee.

He had told her about the man as they drove to Noordwijk and she had been careful to be interested and ask all the right questions and laugh with him over their early morning swim. And at the hotel they lunched off lobster and an enormous salad while Katrina took care to keep their talk light and impersonal, and still keeping it up as he drove north, leaving the main road each time a signpost showed the way to the sea and another small seaside resort, with the wide sands stretching as far as the eye could see and the sea, very blue beyond. The freak wind had died down and it was pleasantly warm, and at Egmont-aan-zee they stopped to eat ices on the terrace of the lido restaurant and then, as a concession to Katrina being English, had tea as well. They were on the coast road now and stayed on it until they reached Alkmaar, where they lingered to look at the magnificent church and inspect the cheese market and the Waaggebouw, where the cheeses were weighed each Friday market day, and since it was a sight not to be missed, they waited until the hour struck so that she might see the gilded figures prancing round the clock tower.

Katrina, very much taken by all that she had seen, chatted lightheartedly on as Raf drove across the polderland to join the main road running down to Amsterdam; the Ijsselmeer on one side of them, the neat farms on the other, but he didn't go to Amsterdam, skirting it and taking the motorway between the city and Haarlem until they reached Leiden. The quiet little country road at the end of their journey was quite empty of traffic and serene under the clear early evening sky. The house looked just as serene as they went up the drive and Katrina said suddenly after a quite long silence:

'What a beautiful home you have, Raf. How you must love coming back to it each time you go away.'

He sounded very casual. 'Yes, and more so than ever before.'

She kept her own voice casual too. 'Oh, why's

that?'

She was disappointed at his: 'I'm getting older, I feel the need to put down roots.'

They were getting out of the car when he stopped to add: 'It's your home too, Kate.'

She hadn't known what she had hoped he would say, so she couldn't quite understand why she should feel so forlorn. She told herself angrily that she would have to do better than that if their future was to be the pleasant calm life Raf so obviously expected, and—patience, she cautioned herself; even though he may never love you he may grow fond of you over the months—years, perhaps.

They went indoors and presently had dinner together and then spent an hour or so playing the record player. Katrina, curled up in a deep chair, listened to Sibelius's Symphony Number 5, and Prokofiev's *Romeo and Juliet*, found them almost more than she could bear; that kind of music always made her feel sentimental, full of longing for something or other, sad . . . She watched Raf, sitting in his chair, legs stretched out before him, smoking a cigar with his eyes shut, or at least she wasn't quite sure if they were shut or not.

They weren't, for presently he asked: 'Why are you looking at me, Kate?'

She became flustered at once. 'Oh, was I? Not looking at you, really, just—just . . .'

'I happened to be in the way?' he suggested placidly.

'Yes, that's it.' She rushed on feverishly: 'What a lovely day it's been—thank you for taking me, Raf.' And when he smiled: 'I had no idea that the coast was so lovely—all that sand—and Alkmaar, and—and the farms . . .' She paused, aware that she was babbling.

'I'm glad you enjoyed it. It hardly began well. We must do better next time.'

Her heart lifted at the prospect of a next time. 'Do you often get days free or weekends?'

'When I can fit them in—I haven't bothered too much about them, but now that you are here we must get around a little. I've neglected my friends. When do we go to Britannia's?'

'On Tuesday evening.'

'I've a couple of lectures next week—Amsterdam and Utrecht, would you like to come along? You could have a look round and meet me for lunch—they're both in the morning.'

Katrina tried not to sound eager. 'I'd like that very much, but you promised that I might go to one of your lectures.'

'Did I? Won't you be bored? I lecture in Dutch, you know.'

'I don't mind—it's just that I'd like to be there, if you wouldn't mind.'

'Why should I mind?' He didn't sound very interested and she hurried on, afraid that she was being too interested. 'I'd like to start learning Dutch—is there someone I could go to? Nanny's been a dear, telling me what I ought to say and when, but I expect I ought to have a teacher.'

'I'll see about someone—would you like them to come here or will you drive in to Leiden?'

She had used the Mini, parked in the big garage between the Bentley and a Saab Turbo Jet, and she had been surprised how quickly she had adjusted to the right-hand traffic. 'I'll drive in.'

Raf nodded. 'Good, I must see about getting you a car of your own.'

Katrina looked shocked. 'Raf, there are three in the garage!'

'But none of them yours, Kate.' He smiled at her. 'Would you like a Mini?'

'Oh, yes, please, but really I could use the one that's already there . . .'

He frowned faintly. 'There's one thing we've never talked about in depth,' he observed, 'money. We must make time to go and see my solicitor so that you understand about the estate and so forth—there are several trusts . . .'

Katrina said weakly: 'Oh, are there?' and wondered just what a trust was. She had often wondered, but had never bothered to find out—why should she? She wasn't likely to be involved in one, but now it seemed that she was.

'I'll give you a bird's eye view, though. I have a lot of money, Kate. A good deal of it I inherited, the rest I earn. I own this house, the house in Friesland and a charming little cottage just outside Den Haag—oh, and the flat in London, of course.'

'Good grief!' exclaimed Katrina. 'You must be rich. Not a millionaire?'

'Well, yes.' He had never looked so bland.

'Why didn't you tell me?'

'You asked me that once before and I answered you. Do you find it so very disturbing, Katrina?'

She was honest enough to admit that no, she didn't. 'In fact, it must be quite fun, though I expect you're quite used to it, Raf; you can have everything you want.'

He was examining his shoes carefully. 'Not quite everything,' he said softly. She thought she knew what he meant.

'Oh, Raf, I'm sorry—of course not. No mother and father and brothers and sisters, and no cousins or aunts and uncles—how could I be so thoughtless?' She got up and went to stand in front of him. 'I'm not the same, but I'll do my best to fill the gap, at least, a little of it. And you can share my family.'

He stood up and took her hands in his. 'What a dear girl you are, Kate.' He was staring down at her and she waited for him to go on talking, but after a moment he dropped her hands and said in a quite different voice: 'I've some telephoning to do.'

She was quick to answer her cue. 'And I'm off to bed—all that fresh air,' she spoke gaily, 'and I promised Berthe that I'd inspect the jams and pickles in the morning.'

And what that has to do with it, I don't know, she thought as she went upstairs, but I had to say something, didn't I?

They left at about six o'clock on the Tuesday to drive to Jake and Britannia's home in the Veluwe, near the little town of Hoenderloo.

Katrina, wishing to look her best, had chosen to wear a crêpe-de-chine dress, a honey-coloured pattern on a creamy background; the pearls went very nicely with it. Raf, waiting for her in the drawing-room, gave her a long look. 'Very nice,' he remarked, 'but why have you put your hair up?'

She was surprised. 'Well, I only had it down the other day because I hadn't time to do anything with it. Don't you like it?'

'It's delightful, but a pity to tuck it all away. Are you ready? It's roughly two hours' driving, but I daresay we shall do it in less time.'

It was well within that time as they came in sight of their friends' house. It was a charming gabled place, surrounded by groups of trees and encircled by a wall, and before they reached it its great door was opened and Jake came out to meet them.

Sitting sleepily by Raf some four hours later, on the way home again, Katrina thought about the evening. It had been delightful. Britannia had come hurrying out to meet them in the hall, a square apartment, tiled underfoot and with a branched staircase at the far end, embraced her with every sign of pleasure, kissed Raf and then led the way into the drawing-room. 'We'll have a drink,' she had declared, 'and then we'll go up and see the twins before dinner.'

Katrina had been surprised at their smallness. They looked like two dolls in their cots, but despite their lack of size, they had inherited their parents' good looks. She had been quite unaware of the wistful expression on her face as she bent over them, nor had she seen Raf's eyes watching her so intently.

The evening had been lighthearted and the dinner delicious, Katrina and Britannia, leaving the men to their port, went back to the drawing-room to chat cosily about babies, the beauty of their houses, their splendid husbands, the clothes they intended to buy and then back to babies. The men joined them presently and they had talked about everything under the sun and when they at last got up to go, Katrina did so with regret, mitigated by the prospect of seeing her new friends again very soon; Raf had suggested a dinner party; it was time, he said, that they had a few friends for the evening and if Jake and Britannia came it would make things easier for Katrina. When he had mentioned it earlier, she had supposed that they would invite two or three of his closest friends, now it seemed there were to be twelve at least. She thought about it on their way home, already worrying about the food and what she should wear and not knowing anyone except the Lutingh van Thiens, but she was too sleepy to talk to Raf about it; tomorrow she would get a list of who was to come and when, from him, and he would have to tell her about them.

It was the evening before she saw him again. When she got down to breakfast the next morning it was to find that he had left an hour earlier; something urgent at the hospital in Leiden, Caspel thought, and he would try to telephone her during the day. It was a brief call when it came, though, merely saying that he was sorry that he had to leave early and that she wasn't to expect him to lunch and that he was bringing an old friend back for dinner.

Katrina went happily enough through her day. There were the dogs to walk, the flowers to do, a visit to the village shop to buy postcards, letters to write and a long afternoon in the pool and then sunbathing.

She went to change in good time. Raf usually came home about six o'clock, but perhaps this evening he would be early. She put on a cream silk jersey dress, sleeveless and simply cut. It was a splendid foil for the pearls and her ring and because Raf had said that he liked it she washed her hair and allowed it to hang loose, curling on to her shoulders. Pleased with her appearance and feeling happy, she went downstairs to wait in the drawing-room, and because she was impatient to see Raf she went to sit in one of the wide window seats, so that she could get a good look at him as he came into the house.

She was looking forward to the evening; she had arranged a delightful dinner, seen to it that the table in the dining-room shone with glass and silver and the white napery Raf liked and made sure that the drinks were ready on the sofa table in the drawing-room: Raf would see to the wine when he got in. She let out a little sigh of pure pleasure as the Bentley came up the drive and got to her feet.

Raf got out and rather to her surprise went round to the other door and opened it. A woman got out; a slim willowy creature, not too tall and beautifully proportioned, her golden hair dressed in an elaborate coil on the top of her head, laughing up at Raf as she stood beside him. She was wearing black, some soft stuff which floated about her and made her more willowy than ever. Katrina stood staring, temper rising slowly. Raf could have warned her that it was a woman guest, given her some idea whom she was to expect. But he hadn't, had he? Her head was already full of half-formed thoughts. Was this the reason why he hadn't come home to lunch or for that matter why he had left so early that morning? Katrina left the window and turned a welcoming, smiling face in the general direction of the door.

They came in together, smiling and at ease and obviously liking each other's company, and Katrina crossed the room to meet them, her lovely eyes glittering with anger. She turned a cheek to receive Raf's casual kiss, said: 'Hullo, dear,' a little too loudly and turned to their guest.

Older than I am, she thought, but loaded with charm, and held out a hand.

'Katrina, this is Beyke. We've known each other for most of our lives, but don't often meet.' He turned to Beyke. 'Two years, is it? How time flies! She landed at Schipol at seven o'clock this morning and the least I could do was meet her.'

Beyke laughed gently and he added: 'This is Katrina, my wife.'

The two shook hands and murmured the usual nothings. She wasn't pretty, Katrina decided, but very, very attractive, which was worse. Her clothes were beautiful too and she made Katrina feel too large. In Raf's company she tended to forget her size because he was much bigger, anyway; and why hadn't he said that he was going to collect a friend from the airport? Why all the secrecy? Her thoughts, behind a smiling face, were hidden, but Raf, watching her, knowing her better than she knew herself, smiled faintly.

'Beyke is just back from the States,' he observed. 'You've been away too long, Beyke.'

Beyke shot him a look which seemed to imply that she agreed with him, and Katrina looked away, feeling murderous. The woman had a lovely voice too, soft and very beguiling . . .

'Well, that's obvious, isn't it? Marrying behind my back, Raf!' She added something in Dutch and Raf laughed and then as though he had just remembered that Katrina was there too and didn't understand Dutch, translated:

'Beyke says that if she had known I was going to settle down at last, she would have come back sooner.'

Katrina, wishing to crown her husband with something suitably heavy, achieved a bright smile. 'Well, it's nice that you're here now, Beyke—I hope we'll see a lot of you,' she added mendaciously. And while Raf was getting their drinks: 'You must have such a lot to talk about. Your English is marvellous, but do speak Dutch if you'd rather, I don't mind in the least.'

'You see what a paragon I have married,' observed Raf blandly as he came back with the drinks. 'She not only swims like a fish, runs the house like clockwork, shares my breakfast each day, but likes all my friends on sight. Was ever a man so blessed?'

Beyke said something softly in Dutch and he grinned and said: 'I shan't translate that, Katrina, you might get a swelled head.'

She smiled her empty smile again, wishing with all her heart that she could understand

Dutch.

They went into dinner presently and Katrina laid herself out to be a superb hostess; it was amazing what one could do when one tried, she mused, listening with every sign of interest to Beyke's witty talk. She might be the wrong side of thirty, but that was the only thing against her, and probably that didn't matter. Raf was thirty-eight . . .

She poured coffee in the drawing-room with a steady hand and then strolled round the garden with their guest while Raf made some telephone calls. They had reached the swimming pool when Beyke observed: 'I had every intention of marrying Raf, but I was offered this terrific job in the States and I went—you see, he seemed to be a more or less confirmed bachelor and I thought he would be safe to leave for a couple of years.' She made a delightful face and then laughed. 'That'll teach me, won't it? All of a sudden he sees you and here I am, left high and dry.' She sighed so heavily that Katrina felt bound to ask:

'Do you love him very much?'

Beyke shrugged. 'Oh, I'll get over it. It is a pity that he is a man who takes marriage seriously, otherwise I might prise him loose.' She gave a trill of laughter and Katrina, at boiling point, laughed too, and then asked in what she hoped was a pleasant friendly voice: 'Where do you live? Raf didn't say . . .'

'Oh, Den Haag—I have a flat there. You must come and see it—Raf knows the way. I haven't got a car yet, such a nuisance, but Raf will drive me back.'

The Hague was no distance away, so why was Raf two hours getting there and back? Katrina lay in bed, fuming until she heard the car go past under her windows. She heard Raf come upstairs presently and go to his room, but she had no desire to sleep, instead she bunched her pillows comfortably and sat back, going over the evening. She hoped she had behaved exactly as Raf would expect. Of course, he hadn't heard all the things that wretched woman had said and his manner towards her had been that of an old friend; Katrina wasn't sure if he had been pleased when she had invited Beyke to join them at the dinner party. She had explained that she didn't know who was coming yet, but she was sure that Beyke would like to meet the other guests, and when she had urged Raf to persuade Beyke to come, he had done so with every appearance of pleasure. All the same, she fancied he had been taken by surprise.

She greeted him briskly the next morning, her cheerful voice belying her pale face, bearing all the obvious hallmarks of no sleep, and as soon as she had sat down with her coffee she cut ruthlessly into the reading of his letters.

'Raf, may I have a list of guests for the dinner party? You did suggest the end of next week and they ought to be invited . . .'

He lifted his eyes from the letter in his hand. 'I'll let you have it at lunchtime, Katrina. Will that do? They're all old friends and won't mind short notice. We'll have to find a man for Beyke . . .'

Katrina scalded her tongue on her coffee and

put the cup down carefully.

'Find a man for me,' she suggested, keeping her voice down with an effort, 'then Beyke can have you all to herself.'

She picked up the cup again and burnt her tongue once more, for Raf had put his letter down and was looking at her so ferociously that she felt the stirrings of fright. 'And what exactly do you mean by that, Katrina?' His voice was so suave and soft that just for a moment she imagined she had dreamed the fierce look on his face. But only for a moment; he was looking at her steadily, and just for once he had lifted his lids so that she saw how bright blue his eyes were and how cold.

She said weakly: 'Well, nothing really— just . . .'

'A joke?' he prompted. 'If it was, it was in very poor taste.' He picked up his letters and got up. 'I've just remembered, I shan't be able to come home to lunch after all, and I'll probably be late home this evening.'

Katrina could think of nothing to say; she'd been a fool, but she mustn't make it worse. Silence is golden and all that, and on no account cry.

She said to his retreating back: 'It's the lecture tomorrow morning, Raf, the one you said I might attend.'

He had stopped and turned round to look at her. 'I hadn't forgotten. Amsterdam at nine o'-clock at the Binnenhof. We shall have to leave here at eight-fifteen, it's only thirty miles, but we may get held up by the traffic.'

'I'll be ready,' said Katrina meekly.

She spent a wretched day doing all the things she had learned to enjoy and now found quite pointless—taking dogs for a walk, arranging a bowl of flowers in the hall, talking to Berthe about food, swimming in the pool, a little gossip with Nanny . . . The day was endless, and at eight o'clock with no sign of Raf and no message either, she sat down to a solitary dinner. It was a couple of hours later, as she sat pretending to read a book, that Raf came home. He looked tired and out of temper, greeted her abruptly and went to get himself a drink.

'Would you like dinner?' asked Katrina. 'I asked Berthe . . .'

'Thanks, no—I had a sandwich. You've had a pleasant day?'

He had flung himself into his chair.

'Me?' She reflected on its arid wasted hours. 'Oh, very nice, thank you. You've been busy?'

'Yes,' he fished in his pocket. 'Here is the list of people I thought we might invite—I got my secretary to type it out. She's enclosed an invitation written in Dutch for you to copy.'

'How thoughtful of her. Will you thank her from me?'

He said suddenly: 'Katrina, about last night—Beyke . . .'

She wouldn't be able to bear it; the creature had been on her mind all day and now he wanted to talk about her. It was too much. She got up so suddenly that her book slipped on to the floor. 'Raf, I'm so sorry, but I've got a headache—I would have gone to bed early, but I wanted to be here when you got home, just in case there was anything you needed.'

He said blandly: 'But, my dear, there are servants enough to see to my needs.' He stood up. 'Don't let me keep you a moment longer. Will your headache prevent you coming in the morning?'

She beat a retreat to the door and found him beside her. 'No—no, it will be perfectly all right by then. Goodnight, Raf.'

He didn't wish her goodnight, but said something in Dutch, and it sounded as though he were laughing.

CHAPTER EIGHT

KATRINA was early for breakfast, but Raf was already there. He wished her good morning and hoped that her headache had gone and she told him mendaciously that yes, thank you, it had, reflecting the while that one's sins always found one out; on the previous evening she had pleaded a headache she hadn't got and now she had a bad one, the result of a poor night's sleep, and had to deny it. Several cups of coffee helped and once they were in the car, driving through the clear sunny morning, she began to feel better. It was going to be a warm day, and she was wearing the striped voile again, high-heeled sandals and their matching shoulder bag. Getting into the car, she had a moment of doubt; Raf was wearing a grey suit, silk shirt and a richly subdued tie; he looked every inch the professor, self-assured, a little aloof, brilliantly clever but modest about it . . . .

'Should I have worn a hat and gloves and sensible shoes?' Katrina glanced down at the green kid sandals.

Raf's eyebrows rose. 'I can't think why, but do tell me.'

'Well, you—you look just as a professor of surgery should look—clever and confident and beautifully tailored . . .'

He said smoothly and without conceit; 'But I am all those things. Why the hat?'

'Well, wouldn't it be more suitable—the professor's wife, you know.'

'Am I to understand that I am a suitable partner for a female in a hat and sensible shoes? Is my image so staid and middle-aged?'

'Of course not!' She hurried to answer him: she had made it sound all wrong, somehow. 'You're neither and you must know it. What I meant was that I'm not elegant enough for you.' Despite herself the words came tumbling out. 'It ought to be someone like—like Beyke.'

'Beyke seems to be rather on your mind.' His voice was silky.

'Well, she's not, but she's on yours ... you wanted to talk about her yesterday evening, but I don't want to know.' She added snappily: 'And I have no wish to quarrel.'

Raf said very evenly: 'In any case, I'm afraid we haven't the time—I don't like to keep the students waiting.'

If Katrina could have had her way, she would have sat silent for the whole journey, but Raf talked as though nothing had happened, making himself agreeable with remote courtesy; as though she were someone he didn't know very well and didn't like over-much, to be tolerated because good manners demanded it.

She sat almost silent, wishing that the day could begin again, that she could unsay the things she had said. And they had been doing so well, too, even before she discovered that she loved him, she had felt happy and content, determined to make a success of things. She wondered miserably if she hadn't fallen in love with him, if she would have minded Beyke turning up. Probably not. The least she could have done would have been to listen to what he had had to say on the previous evening, now he knew her for a jealous ill-tempered creature; probably he already felt resentful that he was tied to her for the rest of his life. After all, he had never said that he loved her; indeed, he had told her that he believed he was past falling in love—the first fine rapture of love, he had said, and he had included her, too. But that wasn't to say that he hadn't been in love, still loved—but for some reason couldn't marry and decided on the second best; an amiable wife, a comfortable relationship with someone who was just as glad as he was to settle for deep liking and compatibility . . .

She would have to get back on to their original friendly footing and bury her love so deep that no one would ever know it. And she would start now, this very minute. 'Raf——' she began in a small voice.

She was cut short by his cheerful: 'Here we are, and there is my registrar waiting for us—he'll look after you.'

She was being ushered out of the car before she could utter another word, introduced to Hans Penningvester, told that she would be picked up after the lecture, and left, to watch Raf disappear through a side door of the hospital.

The registrar was very careful of her, rather as though she were made of something easily broken. He escorted her to a seat in the middle of the lecture hall, but not too near the front, and in his turn introduced her to an older man, whose name she didn't catch.

'I'm so sorry,' she said as she settled in her chair, 'I didn't get your name,' she added apologetically: 'I find Dutch names a bit difficult.'

'Klaus von Donegan, Baroness.' He had a nice rugged face and a friendly smile. 'Do you want me to translate the Professor's lecture, or can you understand Dutch?'

'Almost nothing, but it doesn't matter, I just wanted to come along and hear him.' She gave him a brilliant smile and turned to the registrar. 'May I call you Hans?' she asked him. 'And what happens after the lecture?'

'I take you to the consultants' room, Baroness, and the Professor will be there.'

'Oh, good. He hasn't got any rounds or anything?'

He looked a little surprised and she realised that very likely a husband would tell his wife things like that, so she added: 'I expect the Professor told me, but I've forgotten.'

'No rounds today, but I believe he has private patients this afternoon.'

Katrina looked as though she already knew that. 'Oh, yes, I'd forgotten that too.'

She took a quick look round the hall. It was full now and even as she looked everyone got to their feet and Raf walked on to the platform. She almost burst with pride and love at the sight of him; she wanted to wave and shout that she was there, watching him, but instead she sat primly down with everyone else in the respectful hush.

The registrar whispered that he was lecturing

on end-to-end anastomosis and then sat back, his arms folded across his chest, the picture of attention. Katrina stole a glance at her neighbour on her other side. He was obviously going to give whatever Raf had to say, his closest attention too. Katrina put on a listening face and hoped she looked intelligent.

But it was wonderful just listening to Raf's voice delivering whatever he was delivering in succinct phrases and in tones which compelled attention. She listened to every word and didn't understand one of them.

And afterwards, when the clapping had ceased and Raf had gone, she allowed herself to be led through the hospital to the consultants' room, where she, outwardly composed and never mind how she felt inside, was introduced to half a dozen learned-looking gentlemen who chatted to her in a dignified way, hoped that they would have the pleasure of meeting her frequently, and expressed the opinion that Raf was a lucky devil. A pity Raf didn't seem to feel that he was.

He came to her presently and said in just the right tone: 'We should be going, my dear—I'm afraid that I have several patients to see this afternoon, and if we're going to lunch . . .'

Katrina made her adieux gracefully and finding Hans and Klaus van Donegan in the entrance hall, stopped to thank them for their services before getting into the Bentley with Raf.

'I enjoyed the lecture,' she told him brightly as the car swept through the gateway into the main street.

He gave her a sidelong glance. 'Indeed? Without understanding a word of it? Or did Klaus translate?'

'No—I just enjoyed it.'

He didn't pursue the matter further. 'We'll have to have a quick lunch, I'm afraid,' he observed. 'I've several patients to see this afternoon. I'm sorry.'

He didn't sound particularly sorry, but she murmured that of course it didn't matter in the least, and would he rather drive straight back home, or better still, could she not catch a train or something.

He didn't bother to explain the trains to her, merely said that no, he had ample time to drive her back provided they didn't linger over their meal.

He took her to Dikker en Thijs—the Café du Centre—where they had a delicious and very expensive lunch, served with unobtrusive speed, and then he drove her back, talking pleasantly to her in much the same manner, she guessed, in which he would talk to someone he hadn't met before and wasn't likely to meet again. Peeping at his grave, handsome profile, she decided that she was a little in awe of him. He did everything so well; gave lectures as though he had delivered them since the day he was born, drove a car through thick traffic without so much as tutting once, and despite his prominence in the profession, was almost retiring in his manner. It was the same when they ate out, she had discovered. Waiters rushed to serve him and when he ordered wine, he knew exactly what he wanted; its name, the year . . . and she, who had been reared in a household where the sherry, though a good one, was seldom produced unless there were guests and where claret was served with Sunday lunch and never on a weekday, found it nothing less than miraculous that he should have such a vast knowledge of wines and never boast about it. But he didn't boast, not about anything; if she hadn't attended his lecture that morning she would never have known how important he was.

He didn't get out of the car when they arrived at the house, merely leant across her and opened the door and told her that he hoped to be home about tea time, so she thanked him quickly and went indoors at once as the car rushed back down the drive. Probably, if Raf hadn't said that he would take her to lunch in Amsterdam, he would have brought her home sooner, but he wasn't a man to break his word, even for a lunch which neither of them had really enjoyed.

Katrina felt restless once she was indoors; she took the dogs for a run in the garden and then went to tap on Nanny's door. They had become friends already. Katrina went each day to see how the old lady did, taking care to go during the day, for she knew that Raf spent half an hour with Nanny each evening and he had never suggested that they might go together. Nanny was glad to see her. Her rooms opened on to the verandah which in turn led down easy steps to the garden, and today she was sitting in an upright chair at the top of the steps. Katrina perched on the top of them and began to tell the old lady about the lecture.

Nanny nodded her old head in a satisfied way,

'I always knew he'd be a success,' she said breathily. 'Such a clever boy, he was, and so determined. He used to say to me: "Nanny, am I like my papa?" and I'd say, "Yes, just the same," and he'd be happy.' Nanny cast a quick glance at Katrina. 'I was getting to think he'd never marry, my dear.'

'Well, he must have had lots of opportunities,' Katrina hurried on in what she hoped was a casual manner. 'That lady who came last evening—Beyke something or other—she's so beautiful, Nanny, and an old friend. If I were a man, I'm sure I'd fall for her.'

'Oh, well, I suppose he did, just for a little while,' said Nanny comfortably, 'years ago, that was, and he soon came round, though I'm not so sure about her. Scheming baggage,' Nanny added darkly.

'But I expect she's married since then,' suggested Katrina cunningly.

'That she had, and divorced the poor man—someone from foreign parts, it was. That's why she's back in Holland—looking for someone else to get her claws into, I've no doubt. A good thing Master Raf's married, he'd be just what she's looking for—handsome and successful and more money than he knows what to do with.' She smiled at Katrina. 'He couldn't have chosen a better wife—such a handsome pair you make. I'll be too old to nanny the children, of course, but it'll be nice to see them. And that reminds me, ma'am, I've a niece, not so young, neither, been a nanny until she married and now she's widowed and none of her own—she'd do very well for you once you get started on a family.'

Katrina looked away across the garden with its wide lawns and beds bright with flowers—a splendid garden for children, safe and wide, and the swimming pool enclosed with a good stout gate to keep little people out. Little Rafs with their father's good looks and powerful noses, plaguing the lives out of their little sisters . . .

'That would be ideal, Nanny,' she said dreamily.

'A family,' went on Nanny, happily. 'There's nothing like it—Master Raf never had the chance, poor boy, all the more reason to make up for it with children of his own.' She shot a quick glance at Katrina. 'Of course, you've only been married for a few weeks.'

Katrina turned to face the old lady and achieved a smile. 'Yes—it seems longer than that, somehow. Nanny, you're tired, aren't you? Shall I help you indoors and ring for tea?'

She had tea with Nanny, listening to her talking about Raf when he was a very little boy and how good he had been to her after the war when she had been traced at last. Katrina listened to every word while at the back of her mind she was rehearsing what she would say to Raf when he got home.

But she had no chance to utter any of her carefully planned speeches. Raf didn't come home, instead there was a message to say that he had gone to Utrecht to see an urgent case and would she not wait dinner for him. So she ate alone and then went to read a book until it grew so late that she was forced to go to bed. Caspel, wishing her

goodnight, assured her that he would remain up
for another hour and if the Professor wasn't back
by then, he would see that a tray with suitable
refreshments was left out. But long after the old
man went to bed, Katrina lay awake. It was the
early hours of the morning before she heard Raf's
quiet tread on the stairs. Only then did she allow
herself to go to sleep.

She tried, during the next couple of days, to
talk to Raf. She wanted to apologise for the
things she had said about Beyke, she wanted to
tell him that she hadn't meant to vex him, that
she hoped that they could resume their easygoing
relationship and forget all about it, and she
wanted to say, too, that she had no intention of
prying into things that were no concern of hers.
Which wasn't quite true, but anything to penetrate the placid politeness with which he now
treated her.

He gave her no chance, and she was no match
for him either. He had the ability, she discovered,
of being able to avoid talking about something in
such a way that there was no getting round it.
She didn't even know if he was annoyed with her,
but of one thing she was sure: he had put a bar-
rier between them.

Everyone who had been invited to dinner had
accepted. Katrina, anxious to have everything
perfect, spent a good deal of time with Berthe
with Caspel translating for them both, discussing
the all-important question of food. She settled for
consommé Madrilène, salmon cutlets Mornay,
crown roast of lamb with saffron rice and then,
since strawberries were to be had, a meringue

gateau, topped with lashings of cream. And this being settled to her satisfaction, she spent the rest of the morning arranging the flowers for the dining-room; a great Delft bowl full of pink roses on a side table and a smaller silver rose bowl cunningly heaped with honeysuckle, lilies of the valley, roses in various shades of pink and pale coloured stocks, spiced with rosemary and sprigs of mint. It looked charming and smelled delicious. The heavy candelabrum, in the baroque style and fashioned in silver-gilt, had been polished to perfection by Caspel, as had the table silver, and Katrina, mindful of Raf's preference for white linen, had searched the great linen cupboard until she found a damask cloth and matching napkins, and then, her heart in her mouth in case something was smashed, decided on using the Weesp porcelain dinner service, preserved intact since the end of the eighteenth century. Caspel, helping her to sort out what was needed, told her that it hadn't been used for some time—special occasions, he said, weddings and christenings and so on.

'Well,' said Katrina a shade defiantly, 'I consider this is an important occasion—our first dinner party! And Caspel, don't let anyone wash the dishes, will you? When everyone's gone, I'll come down to the kitchens and do them. You can dry, if you like, but I'll take the responsibility.'

'But, Baroness, you must not . . .,' began Caspel.

'No one need know,' she told him bracingly.

She went to dress in good time. Raf, who should have been home about five o'clock, hadn't yet returned, nor had he telephoned. Katrina pondered the advisability of telephoning the hospital and decided against it; it smacked of fussing, something which she knew he couldn't tolerate. Something urgent would have held him up, but obviously he would be able to get home in time, otherwise he would surely have let her know.

She didn't allow herself to worry about it as she dressed. She had taken the Mini in to Leiden on the previous day and bought a new dress—a piece of extravagance which took—for a brief period at any rate—her mind off her troubles. It was a misty blue and green pattern in organza with a wide neckline and long tight sleeves, and she knew that she looked good in it. And since it was an important occasion, to her at any rate, she wore the pearls and put her hair up into a chignon.

The house was quiet when she went downstairs and into the drawing-room. She sat down and picked up her needlework, wondering if a drink would help her to get rid of the apprehension she was feeling. She went over the dinner arrangements once more and found them quite perfect. She hadn't missed a single detail, of that she was quite sure, so the scary feeling must be something to do with Raf.

It was. She hadn't been sitting for more than five minutes when she heard the Bentley sweeping up the drive. She flung down her work and went to one of the windows, just in time to see Raf get out of the car and go round to open the door for his passenger. Katrina knew who it was before the door was fully opened—Beyke, looking glamorous in black chiffon and looking up at Raf

as though she were sharing some delightful secret
... Katrina ground her teeth and went back to
her chair. She was stitching with apparent calm
when the door opened and Raf and Beyke came
in. The look of surprise she gave them was very
well done, even though it didn't deceive Raf for
one moment. He smiled at her gently, looking at
her through half shut eyes. 'Hullo, my dear—I'm
very late, but I really couldn't get away earlier—
and since I was so delayed it seemed a good idea
to fetch Beyke on the way.'

'Why, of course.' Katrina exchanged a social
kiss with her guest. 'What a good idea. Do come
and sit down—we'll have a drink while Raf's
changing.'

Raf went to the sofa table. 'Whisky for you,
Beyke? Sherry for you, Katrina?' He had a hand
on the decanter when she said quickly:

'I'll have a whisky too, thank you, Raf.'

She never drank the stuff, but she needed a
stiff drink. Raf, bringing them their glasses, hid a
smile behind his placid face. 'I'll take mine with
me,' he observed. 'I'll be fifteen minutes.'

It seemed like fifteen hours to Katrina, chatting brightly about clothes and the weather and
Beyke's numerous men friends. 'None of them
can equal Raf, of course,' she said carelessly, 'but
I suppose I'll have to make do. Some of us have
been planning a couple of weeks on the Riviera,
and I suggested that you both might like to join
us. Raf's got a couple of weeks free at the end of
August—it shouldn't be too bad then, although
the spring is the best time to go, don't you agree?'

'I wouldn't know. I've never been.'

Beyke's eyebrows rose. 'No? My dear, what can you have been doing with yourself all these years?'

'Working in London. I always went home for holidays, it made a nice change.'

'You poor dear!' The smile was a charming one and as cold as ice. 'Could I have another whisky?'

Katrina gave herself another one too. The first had gone to her head straight away, heaven alone knew what the second one would do—send her flat on her face, probably. Not that it would matter, she had no doubt that her companion would step into her shoes and play the hostess with grace and charm. She turned a slightly flushed face to her husband as he came into the room. 'Beyke's been telling me about this scheme for a holiday on the Riviera . . .'

If the whisky hadn't had such a peculiar effect upon her, she might have noticed the look of surprise, instantly gone, on his face, and if she had looked at their guest, she would have seen the sudden dismay on that lady's beautiful features. It was perhaps fortunate that the great door bell clanged at that moment and Raf went into the hall to meet the first of their guests.

Outwardly, the evening was a success. The dinner was excellent, and Katrina, still slightly woolly from the whisky, nevertheless played her part well. It was Britannia who came to sit with her for a few moments in the drawing-room after dinner, and whispered: 'Your eyes are glittering—are you in a rage?'

'Yes—oh, dear, does it show?'

'No, everyone is saying how lovely you are and

what a marvellous hostess . . .' Britannia paused and went on in a much louder voice: 'It's such a lovely colour, Katrina—just right with your colouring. Where did you get it?'

One of the partners' wives had joined them, a pleasant little woman with not much to say for herself, but she had a sweet face and a complete lack of ill-nature. The three of them talked clothes until the men joined them.

Everyone began to leave about eleven o'clock, showing a flattering reluctance to do so. Britannia and Jake were getting into their car when Beyke swam into the hall, a filmy wrap over her dress. She stood on the steps between Raf and Katrina, watching them, and Jake, on the point of getting in, said: 'Would you like a lift? We can drop you off.'

Beyke tucked an arm into Raf's. 'How sweet of you, but Raf's taking me.'

Katrina didn't look, but stood smiling woodenly at Britannia, which was a pity, for if she had done so, she would have seen Raf gently remove Beyke's hand.

Raf didn't go back into the house. 'I'll get the car,' he said cheerfully, and walked off round the side of the house in the direction of the garage, leaving Katrina to make bright conversation until he returned, ushered Beyke into the seat beside him and with a casual salute, drove off.

Katrina went back into the house then, suppressing a desire to bolt the doors so that Raf wouldn't be able to get in when he got back. And when would that be? she wondered. She was halfway up the stairs when she remembered that she had promised to wash the Weesp china.

Caspel was waiting for her in the kitchen, and what was more, he had thoughtfully made a pot of tea for her. 'Caspel, you're an angel,' she told him. 'How did you know?'

'The Professor told me that you very much liked your tea, Baroness, and it seemed to me that a cup might refresh you.'

Katrina kicked off her slippers and drank two cups and then, wrapped in one of Berthe's aprons, started on the china, washing each piece with the utmost care and laying it on a thick cloth to drain. She was on the last few pieces when the kitchen door opened and Raf asked mildly: 'Now why are you doing that, Kate?'

She put down the plate in her hand very carefully. 'I wasn't sure if you would mind me using the Weesp dinner service,' she told him in a voice she strove to keep matter-of-fact, 'and it seemed only fair to wash it up myself, then if I smashed any of it, you could blame me.'

'Something I would never do, Kate. It was an inspiration to use it, the table looked delightful.' He strolled over to where Caspel stood, tea towel in hand, and took it from him. 'Caspel, go to bed, and thank you. I'll help the Baroness and if we smash anything, we can share the blame.'

Caspel wrung his elderly hands. 'It is not possible,' he began, 'that you should wash the dishes. It is not fitting . . .'

'It makes a nice change, Caspel—and thank Berthe for her splendid cooking, will you? Everything was delicious.' Raf picked up a small dish. 'Goodnight, Caspel.'

And, 'Goodnight, Caspel,' echoed Katrina. She washed the last plate, emptied the sinks, wiped them clean, and went over to the big scrubbed table and began to stack the porcelain carefully on to two trays, and while she did it she tried to think of something to say.

'If you go ahead and open the cabinet doors, I'll bring the trays up,' observed Raf pleasantly.

The cabinet was in one of the long wide corridors on the ground floor, a huge walnut piece, with bow-fronted glass doors. She had them open as Raf appeared with the first of the trays. It took them ten minutes to house the precious stuff and when Raf closed the door and locked it Katrina let out a sigh of relief. 'I've been on tenterhooks the whole evening,' she admitted, 'in case something got smashed.'

'Is that why you drank two whiskies before dinner?' asked Raf silkily.

She was too tired to think of a clever answer. It was ironic that now, when they were alone together, undisturbed, she found herself unable to say any of the things she would have liked to. She said merely: 'I was nervous—it was my first dinner party and I wanted it to be a success.' She found herself hoping that he would praise her and perhaps even say that her dress had been pretty.

'I can't imagine why it should have been anything else but a success.' He was leaning against the cabinet, his hands in his pockets, looking at her. 'You're a very capable girl and you have plenty of help.' He turned away. 'I think we had better go to bed, don't you?'

Katrina stayed where she was choked with rage. 'Yes, I do.' She took a breath. 'I'm surprised you're back so quickly.'

He had turned to look at her. 'I had no reason to loiter,' he said evenly.

She was beside herself, not really caring what she said now. 'No, I don't suppose you had, you had had plenty of time to tell Beyke how lovely she looked in that dress and how pretty her hair was . . .'

She took a step backwards because Raf was suddenly close to her, his hands on her shoulders. 'And is that what you want of me?' he asked. 'That I should tell you that you were the loveliest woman in the room? That none of them could hold a candle to you? That your hair shone like silk in the candlelight? And if I did, would you believe me?'

Katrina felt the tears prick her eyes. 'Raf, why didn't you tell me about Beyke? And then seeing his face, bland once more: 'No, it doesn't matter.' She turned and ran down the corridor, out into the hall and up the stairs, into her room. Her slippers were still in the kitchen, but she hadn't given them a thought; indeed, she wasn't thinking at all, she was too unhappy.

CHAPTER NINE

KATRINA might be unhappy, but she wasn't a coward. She got up at the usual time and went down to breakfast, pale and heavy-eyed but quite in command of herself again.

Raf's good morning was pleasant. He looked exactly as he always did, calm and self-contained. He passed her the toast, remarked upon the splendour of the morning and went back to his letters. Only as he was gathering these together preparatory to leaving did he say: 'I find I have a day free this week. I thought we might go up to Friesland and I could show you the house at Waaxburen. I've some business to attend to there as well, but that shouldn't take too long.'

She was so surprised that she stammered a little. 'Oh—I'd like to go v-very much. I won't be in the way?'

She couldn't understand the look he gave her, questioning, amused and something else. 'No, Kate. Would directly after breakfast tomorrow suit you? We'll take the dogs with us, they enjoy the ride.'

Later that morning Katrina went along to see Nanny; the old lady would like to hear about the dinner party, what the women wore, what they ate. She recounted it all faithfully to Nanny and she sighed with pleasure. 'Master Raf, he's a good boy, always tells me everything, but he's no good with dresses and suchlike, not that he doesn't like to see women well dressed. Berthe told me that the evening was a great success and that you looked like a dream. You shouldn't have done the dishes, though, ma'am dear—baronesses shouldn't wash up.'

'Well, here's one that does. What's more, the Baron helped.'

Nanny's old eyes gleamed. 'Did he now? Well, I never did! That was after he took Mevrouw van Teule home, no doubt.'

'Yes.' Katrina didn't want to talk about that. Nothing would have been nicer than to have sat at Nanny's feet and poured out the whole story, but being a wife meant being loyal too. She said cheerfully: 'We're going to the house in Friesland tomorrow. Such a funny name—Waaxburen. Have you been there, Nanny?'

'Oh, yes, and very nice it is too, quite different from this house, of course and very countrified. Master Raf does a good bit of sailing in the summer; it's close to the sea.'

'And a farm too?' prompted Katrina, wanting to know more.

Nanny nodded. 'Friesian cows, sheep and those giant horses—percherons, as well as Friese *ruiters*, I think they're called. It's a big place—not a large farmhouse, but plenty of land. You'll like it there, ma'am dear.'

Perhaps, thought Katrina wistfully, she would have a chance to talk to Raf while they were there; peace and quiet, away from everyone. She couldn't tell him that she loved him, of course, but she could let him see that she really wanted to make their marriage work. Even if it meant accepting Beyke as a friend ... She looked so fierce that Nanny asked her if she was feeling all right.

She did her best at lunch time, trying not to notice Raf's cool courtesy, chatting brightly about the farm and getting brief polite replies. He would be later home that evening, he told her as he went; he had private patients to see and she need not expect him before six o'clock. As an afterthought he asked her what she was doing that afternoon, and she was able to tell him with perfect truth that she was having tea with the partners' wives.

She drove herself in the Mini to Leiden, where they both lived, and spent an hour or two drinking milkless tea and nibbling wafer thin sweet biscuits, listening to their friendly chatter. They were two nice young women, anxious to make her feel at home, laughingly correcting her Dutch when she tried out a sentence or two. She left them about five o'clock and since Raf wasn't coming home until six o'clock, she drove towards the sea and when she reached Noordwijk, parked the car and walked down to the beach.

It was a warm day, but the breeze was strong and she shivered a little as she watched the sun-spangled sea, dotted by sailing boats. It had been exciting, rescuing the injured man and the child. Raf seemed to have forgotten all about it and she had consoled herself by telephoning her mother and telling her the whole story. It had been nice to be praised a little and exclaimed over, just as Nanny, bless her heart, had done—all the same,

Raf might have said something, not taken her for granted. Next time there was a crisis, she told herself, she would take care to faint or scream or do something else entirely feminine.

After a while she turned away from the sea, got back into the car, and drove home, to find Raf already there. He was with Franz, in front of the house, examining the lawns, but when he saw the Mini he came to meet her. 'I finished rather sooner than I expected,' he greeted her. 'I rang Greta's house, but she said that you had already left.' He didn't ask her where she'd been, but she heard the faint question all the same.

'I drove to Noordwijk and had a look at the sea. It was full of sailing boats, and sparkling in the sun . . .' Her voice died away. She wasn't looking at him, but remembering how she had climbed on board the yacht and seen him there, dripping water all over the place, not in the least surprised to see her, demanding splints . . .

'Rather different from our little adventure,' he observed placidly. 'Did I ever tell you how magnificent you were, Kate?'

She felt the tears crowding her throat. 'No, you told me 'I was wet.'

He glanced at her and saw her eyes bright with tears. 'That sounds a little inadequate.'

She had turned away from him. 'No, not in the least—it was quite true.' She had swallowed the tears now and went on: 'I'm going in—I promised Nanny I'd have a chat after tea.'

She didn't care if Raf believed her or not; it was an excuse to get away from him.

Perhaps it was a good thing that he was called

out that evening halfway through dinner. An accident near Utrecht and the two victims had been taken to the hospital there, both needing expert surgery. As he left the table he said quietly: 'I'll try not to be late, my dear, but it sounds like a long business. Don't wait up.'

Katrina went to bed early. The great house seemed so empty without Raf. She wandered through the splendid rooms, loving them, wondering if she would ever feel as though she belonged there. In time, she supposed, if she could come to terms with her new life.

She had been asleep for some hours when she heard the car coming up the drive. It was almost three o'clock; Raf would be tired out and probably hungry. She got out of bed, put on a dressing gown and slippers and went silently downstairs to meet him as he opened the great front door.

'What's the matter?' he asked sharply. 'Are you ill, Katrina?'

She hesitated on the bottom step. 'No, I heard the car and I wondered if you wanted a hot drink and something to eat.'

He was already on his way across the hall, going to his study. 'I had something at the hospital. It was kind of you, but there was no need to come down. Go back to bed and finish your sleep.' He glanced at her briefly. 'Goodnight, Kate.'

She turned without a word and went back to her room, to sit up in bed and worry. There was something not right between them; she had offered such a small service and been thoroughly

snubbed—very nicely, of course, but snubbed.
And he had said before they married that he liked
her—enjoyed her company, that they were com-
patible. They were nothing of the sort; she cried
a little then and presently fell asleep, to wake
heavy-eyed when her morning tea arrived.

But very little of her worries showed on her
face when she went down to breakfast, thanks to
make-up and a determination not to let Raf see
that she was hurt. She wished him a serene good
morning and took a good look at him. He might
not have slept, but excepting for the tired lines of
his face, no one would have guessed it. Fortified
by a cup of hot coffee, she asked: 'Do you have to
go back to Utrecht today, Raf?'

He shook his head. 'No, my registrar can deal
with anything. Both the men who were injured
stand a good chance of recovery.'

'Oh, good. What was wrong?'

He told her while they breakfasted and then
gathered up his letters. 'I'll leave these for Juf-
frouw Kats to deal with. Can you be ready in ten
minutes?'

She had taken the precaution of seeing Berthe
the evening before, so that the meals for the day
had been decided upon. 'Yes. If I could know
roughly what time we'll be back, so that I can let
Berthe know about dinner . . .'

'We'll dine at Waaxburen, that will give us
more time there.'

The journey was just over a hundred miles and
most of it on motorways, with a brief pause for
coffee at Wieringerwerf, they were across the
Afsluitdijk and tearing along the Friesland

countryside well before noon. Raf had turned away from the main road at Franeker, going towards the coast now, through farmland, dotted by farmhouses, their barns built against their back walls, looming high above them. Presently he turned on to a narrow *dijk* road, which wound through two small villages and then disappeared into a belt of trees. The trees opened out presently, on to green fields, surrounded on all sides by more trees, and fenced by tall iron palings. Katrina could see the farmhouse now, standing well back within the protecting circle of trees. There were cattle in the fields surrounding it, and horses, but she lost sight of it all for a moment while Raf turned the car between two great stone pillars almost hidden by trees and shrubs. But on the other side she had a clear view again and she exclaimed with delight.

'Raf, it's beautiful, all those trees and the fields are so green. How you must love it!'

'I do. If I hadn't become a surgeon, I would have chosen to be a farmer.'

'But you like being a surgeon?'

'Oh, yes, I couldn't be anything else—it's in my blood, but I love this place.'

He had stopped the car before the front of the farmhouse and got out. As he opened Katrina's door, a man came out to meet them; a tall sturdy man with greying hair and the same aquiline features as Raf.

The two men shook hands and Raf turned to Katrina. 'My cousin Seles.' He smiled at the man. 'This is my wife, Katrina.'

'I'm so glad to meet you, Katrina.' He had a

nice smile. 'I am a cousin, but not a close one, you understand—we are separated by many uncles and cousins, all, alas, dead.'

'But we bear the same name,' said Raf. He took Katrina's arm and led her indoors, into a square hall, panelled in wood, and a little on the dark side. It was furnished with an old cloak chest, a couple of high-backed chairs, and a wall table with a great deal of carving on it, the whole made cheerful by the copper bowls filled with flowers. The stairs were in one corner, uncarpeted and narrow, polished with age and beautifully carved too. There were three doors leading from the hall and the room they entered was obviously the sitting-room, a large, high-ceilinged room, running from the front of the house to the back and with windows at each end. It was most comfortably furnished with outsize chairs and sofas, covered in tapestry, a number of tables scattered around, shelves of books against one wall, and a variety of paintings on its plain whitewashed walls. There were flowers here too, and Raf said easily: 'I see that Mieke is still as artistic as ever,' to be answered by the woman who had just joined them.

She was not young any more and not pretty, but she had lovely eyes and a sweet smile and she went straight to Katrina. 'You don't have to tell me who this is,' she said to Raf. 'I'd have known her from your description, only she's ten times prettier.' She took Katrina's hand. 'It's lovely to meet you—I'm Mieke, but you'll have guessed that.' She drew Katrina down on to a massive sofa as she spoke. 'Shall we have coffee first, then you two men can talk business and I'll show Katrina the house.'

The men didn't linger, but drank their coffee and left the two of them chatting happily. Mieke had spent several years in England and her English was fluent; they had a son there now, she told Katrina, at one of the agricultural colleges. 'Our other son is still at school, he intends to be a doctor,' she added. 'He'll go to Leiden, of course, and Pieter, the eldest, is going to farm in Groningen. Raf has a small farm there too—I expect you know that, he promised it to Pieter some years ago, good kind generous man that he is. This farm isn't ours, you see, it's Raf's, but we've lived here for years now and run it for him. He comes here a great deal and takes a great interest in it, but it's ours for our lifetime. Between us we've made a great success of it, I think. Come and see the house.'

There was a dining-room across the hall, furnished ponderously in the Beidermeier style but bright with chintz and flowers, and the kitchen, a large room with a great table in its centre, an Aga cooker and rows of copper pans against one of the walls. There was an old-fashioned dresser too, filled with rows of beautiful old plates and saucers, their matching cups hanging on little brass hooks. There was a door into the garden and another door which led straight into the barn, with its rows of spotless stalls and scrubbed floor. And upstairs there were a number of bedrooms, all furnished with taste and in great comfort, and still higher, up a tiny staircase like a ladder, was a loft running right across the house. There was a table at one end, a darts board on the wall, and a train set arranged on the floor, as well as several comfortable chairs, a T.V. set, a record player and a pile of skates, fishing rods and tennis rackets.

'This was—is—the boys' room. When they're home they come up here and make all the noise they like. I leave it like this because it'll do for your boys when they come up here to stay.' She twinkled at Katrina. 'A bit soon, I know, but here it is ready and waiting.'

Katrina smiled and nodded, thinking sadly that as far as she could see it would go on waiting. 'What's it like in the winter?' she asked, anxious to change the subject.

'Well, cold. We get a good deal of snow and there's usually a chance to skate for at least a few weeks, sometimes longer. Raf always comes just before Christmas, so you'll be able to see it for yourself. Only wear lots of woollies.'

They went back to the sitting room presently and the men joined them for drinks before lunch, a substantial meal of smoked eel, chicken casserole and fruit salad and cream. Katrina, who possessed a good appetite, found that she had none at all, probably because Raf, while treating her with his usual pleasant good manners, somehow contrived to make her feel like a stranger. Perhaps it was something she was imagining, though, for the other two laughed and talked as though she had been in the family for ages.

She wasn't alone with Raf for one single moment for the rest of the day; he was out and about all the afternoon, coming in briefly for a cup of tea and going off again to look at the horses. Katrina, listening to Mieke's cheerful voice, remembered that she had supposed she and Raf would be alone all day. Perhaps on the drive back . . .

They left about nine o'clock after a bountiful dinner and, in Katrina's case, a little bit too much to drink. It had made her feel pot-valiant and once they had waved their last goodbyes and the farm was out of sight she began: 'Raf, there are lots of things I want to say to you, and you must listen. I thought we'd be alone at the farm and I'd made up my mind . . .' She was suddenly overcome with sleep.

She woke up again as they were coming off the Afsluitdijk and turning on to the E10 going down to Amsterdam. 'Oh, where are we?' she wanted to know, her wits still woolly.

'Back in north Holland, just off the Dijk. You've been asleep for almost an hour.' Raf sounded amused.

'Oh, I'm sorry, I didn't mean to go to sleep—dinner was rather much and I had three glasses of claret.'

'You were saying before you slept . . .' Raf's voice was dry.

Katrina sat up and looked around her, gathering courage. The country was pretty in the late evening dusk, but they were rushing along so fast she couldn't see much of it. She glanced at Raf, but their was nothing to learn from his profile. 'I just want to say,' she began carefully, 'that something's gone wrong—I know what it is, you're angry because I—I said that about Beyke. I expect you think I'm jealous, but I'm nc :.' Her voice shook a little over the lie, but she went on steadily: 'When we married I knew that you must have friends of your own, people you'd known long before you met me.' She took a deep breath and rushed on: 'I don't know why . . . that is, I expect if you'd known Beyke wasn't married any more you wouldn't have married me. You told me that you wanted a wife—well, a companion really, and I thought that you were lonely and—and just wanted—well, a companion, like I said, but of course you wanted to forget Beyke, and then she turned up and you could have married her after all.' She added in a very small voice indeed: 'I don't know if you want a divorce.'

Raf didn't answer; he was driving very fast now, tearing down the road, passing everything ahead of him. Presently Katrina said admonishingly: 'You're not frightening me, going fast.'

His harsh laugh made her jump 'Frightened? Which of us is supposed to be frightened?'

Which left her wondering what he had to be frightened about.

He slowed as they reached the outskirts of Amsterdam and then wound through its streets until they joined the motorway to Leiden, less than thirty miles away. It was quite dark now and she couldn't see his face. At last she ventured: 'You haven't said anything.'

'What exactly did Beyke tell you?' he asked in a voice which held no expression at all.

'That you were going to marry, only she went to America and got married there, and when she got back you—you'd married me . . .'

'And of course you believed her.' He sounded

quite friendly again.

'Yes, yes, I think I did. You see, when you brought her home ... you knew each other so well ... Only I wish you'd told me, Raf.'

He said thoughtfully: 'What difference would it make? When I asked you to marry me I made it plain what I wanted, did I not? You can hardly say you lost me, for you are so sure that you never had me.'

Katrina said slowly: 'That's true.'

She was glad of the dark when he spoke again. 'Do you love me, Kate?'

'No, no, I don't.' She spoke too loudly and too quickly. 'So you see it's quite all right for us to be friends again, and I'll do anything you want about Beyke.'

He said very quietly: 'Have we given ourselves a chance, Kate? We've been married such a short time ...'

'Yes, I know, but when we married we didn't know about Beyke—that's altered everything ...' She tried to make her voice eager.

'It seems so.' He had heard the eagerness. He said impassively: 'Perhaps we should allow ourselves a little more time to consider.' He was tooling the car along the narrow road leading to their home. 'I have to go to Vienna tomorrow morning, perhaps we could let the matter stand until I get back.'

'How long will you be gone?'

'Two days. Kage, are you quite sure you don't love me—just a little? It would make all the difference.'

Of course it would. If she said yes, he would

turn his back on Beyke and spent the rest of his life being a good husband. 'No, no, I don't.' She added to clinch the matter: 'I like you very much though.'

'Thanks.' Raf stopped the car before their door and Caspel, although it was long past his bed-time, opened it with a soft-voiced welcome and the offer of hot coffee in the smaller sitting-room. To rush upstairs to her room wouldn't do at all, so Katrina said, 'Oh, Caspel, how thoughtful of you,' and added: 'I'd love a cup.'

They drank their coffee in the pleasant little room, discussing their day just as though their talk in the car hadn't been. Katrina didn't notice that she had burnt her tongue with the scalding coffee, she was so miserable that nothing seemed real; she heard her own voice answering Raf and it sounded quite normal in her ears. She got up presently, thanked him for her lovely day and tried not to see the bitter little smile on his face, wished him goodnight and asked: 'Are you going very early?'

'I'll leave about six o'clock.'

'Oh—then I hope you have a good trip. I'll— I'll see you when you get back.'

Raf stood up too. He looked angry and remote and very tired. It was all the more surprising that he should suddenly be close to her, wrap her in his arms and kiss her hard and long.

The moment he let her go, Katrina flew from the room and up the staircase. She'd never been kissed like that before; she supposed it was a fare-well kiss to their brief marriage. Whatever it was, she wouldn't forget it in a hurry.

She got into bed and cried her eyes out and at last fell asleep, not to wake until Juldou roused her long after eight o'clock with her morning tea. She drank the pot dry, thinking of Raf, already in the air, going miles away from her.

She spent an aimless morning, exercising the dogs, patiently listening to Franz, explaining in basic Dutch so that she could understand him why the peach trees, espaliered on the old brick wall at the end of the kitchen garden, were being sprayed with Bordeaux mixture to destroy peach leaf curl, and then going to the kitchen to tell Berthe that she would have something on a tray for her lunch and would be out for tea. She had no idea where she was going; she would take the Mini and go somewhere—anywhere—away from her unhappy thoughts.

She was pecking at her lunch and listening to the news on the radio when there was a sudden break and another urgent voice took over. There had been a bad plane crash, it said, somewhere in Austria. A morning flight out of Schiphol. The voice gave the flight number and added that as far as was known there were some survivors. Katrina hadn't understood every word, but enough. She flew out of the sitting-room and into Raf's study; when he was away he always left the details of his journey on his desk. The flight number on the memo pad was the same, it seemed to leap from the paper and blind her. She was running back across the hall when she met Caspel, white-faced.

'Caspel, you heard? It's the Professor's flight. Oh, Caspel!' She put a hand on his old arm and

just for a moment was swamped by black despair.
But only for a moment. 'I'll ring Schiphol, they
may know something.' It took a long time to get
through, probably the wires were jammed with
people as anxious as she was. Finally there was a
voice, a kind voice, answering her questions. Yes,
there had been a plane crash, there was a possibility that there were survivors, and when Katrina
asked from a dry mouth if Professor Baron van
Tellerinck had been on the passenger list, the
voice became kinder than ever, and said that yes,
he had, and asked if further information as it
came in should be telephoned through.

Katrina felt very calm now. 'No, thank you.
I'm driving to Schiphol now—if my husband is
one of the survivors, I'll be able to get a flight to
him without delay.'

She stood for a long moment, pushing panic
and fear and a terrible grief on one side so that
she might think clearly. She would need her passport, money, the car. She turned to Caspel
standing by her. 'There may be survivors.' Her
eyes begged him to believe that. 'I'm going to
Schiphol—if necessary I'll get a flight to wherever it is. I could charter a plane . . . Caspel, get
the Mini round for me, will you? I'll be five minutes.'

Her eyes filled with tears, but she dashed them
away and ran upstairs to return within minutes
with a jacket, shoulder bag and passport. Caspel
was standing at the open door, and everyone else
who had anything to do with the house was
standing behind him.

'Perhaps it's not true,' he said, and his eyes

searched her face like a trusting old dog.

'We'll pray it's not, Caspel. I'm not sure if I'm doing the right thing, but I can't just sit here and wait. If there are any messages let me know. If— if I need to fly there I'll telephone you.' She took his hand and squeezed it, then remembered at the last minute to fly along to Nanny's room, to find the old lady sitting in her chair, staring blankly before her.

'It's all right Nanny,' Katrina spoke with false cheerfulness. 'I'm driving over to Schiphol now—they say there are some survivors, so we mustn't give up hope.' She gave her a quick hug. 'Oh, Nanny dear, he must be safe—we all love him so.'

Nanny's face broke into an uncertain smile. 'That's right, dearie. You'll let us know . . ?'

'At once, Nanny.' Katrina dropped a kiss on the elderly cheek and hurried back to the hall. She was conscious of sympathetic voices as she went out of the door and got into the Mini, and she remembered to wave to them all before she stormed down the drive.

The first part of the journey was along a narrow country lane running between water meadows, and there was almost no traffic. Katrina slowed through the village and then sent the little car tearing along the dyke road until a huge farm wagon, lumbering ahead of her, blocked it completely. She crept along behind it, her nerves screaming, shaking with impatience, until it turned into an open gateway and she was able to pass it at last and speed on again until she reached the next village. She was almost at the motorway now; one more village first, though. She could see it ahead of her, a couple of miles away, clearly visible in the flat landscape. She was driving too fast, but she would have to slow down again and the first few cottages were at hand already. The road had a bend in it as she entered the long street of the village and there was a good deal of stationary traffic drawn up on it. Which was why she didn't see the Bentley surging towards her to pass in a flash while she was crawling round an awkwardly parked van.

Raf saw her, though. He had brought the car to a halt, turned it smoothly and was on her tail as she reached the centre of the village. The road curved here, round the church, then straightened out again beyond it, and here it was empty of traffic and quiet as Raf shot the Bentley alongside the Mini and then deliberately crowded the little car on to the grass verge.

Katrina, anxious to pick up speed but vaguely aware that there was a car creeping steadily past her, slowed and shot an impatient glance sideways to see the Bentley's sleek nose alongside with Raf at the wheel. She didn't believe what she saw, not for a second or two, but in that time he had drawn ahead of her, crawling to a stop so that she had to brake hard; even so the Mini crunched into the Bentley's stately back. And before she could move Raf had opened the door, switched off the engine, undone her seat belt and plucked her out of the Mini.

It was when she felt his great arms around her that she began to cry; great gulping sniffs and sobs which he didn't try to stop, only held her close.

'They said you were on the plane,' mumbled Katrina into his shirt front. 'Oh, Raf, I thought you'd been killed and I never told you that I love you, and it doesn't matter if you know now, I don't care any more even though you don't love me. I'll never say it again, I promise I won't, only let me stay with you . . .'

A small number of people, pleased to have something out of the ordinary to stare at, had formed a ragged circle around them but Katrina hadn't noticed, and as for Raf, he didn't care.

'My darling girl, I hope you will say it repeatedly for the rest of our lives together.'

Katrina stopped snivelling. 'Raf—Raf, you don't mind? You want me to love you?' She lifted a sodden face to his and he smiled at her, a slow tender smile to make her poor scared insides glow.

'Why, of course, my dearest darling. If you hadn't been quite so anxious to keep everything on a friendly footing between us, you might have noticed that I've been in love with you since that day we met. What other reason could I have had for marrying you?'

'Yes, but you said . . .'

He bent to kiss her. 'It seemed the quickest way to get you.'

'I didn't love you—not at first.'

'I know that; I began to despair that you ever would, and I was angry too.'

'Because of Beyke?'

'Yes, my love, because you thought that I could treat you in such a way. I went out of my way deliberately to make you think that there was something between us. There never was, you know. Beyke puffed up a mild flirtation ten years ago into an affair because she rather enjoys making mischief. And just for a time I thought it might scare you into realising that you loved me.' He kissed her again and she said dreamily:

'It was on that yacht.'

'My brave girl!' He paused to look at a policeman, getting off his bike and coming towards them. 'Yes, Coulsma?'

'Oh, it's you, Baron.' The man beamed at them both. 'A small accident, perhaps?'

Raf explained while the onlookers murmured sympathy.

'I'll see about the little car, Baron—you'll be wanting to take the Baroness home.'

In an atmosphere of the utmost goodwill, Katrina was helped into the Bentley. She must look a perfect fright, she thought distractedly, but everyone was looking at her so kindly while they told each other what had happened and smiled and waved as Raf started the car. She looked at him too and encountered a look of such love that she almost burst into tears again.

'Everyone's so kind,' she gulped, 'and that nice policeman, too.' And then remembering: 'Raf darling, why didn't you go to Vienna?'

He smiled at her. 'I found I couldn't leave you like that; I couldn't wait two days before seeing you again. I cancelled my lectures and came home determined to make you see that I loved you.' He picked up her hand and kissed it gently and an old lady looking on clapped her hands with delight. 'Let us go home, my darling.' He raised a polite hand in farewell to their audience and drove round the church, back on to the road which would take them home.

The various members of the household, who had been standing about aimlessly, too shocked to do much, had come running at Caspel's news that the Bentley was coming up the drive. They all watched with deep pleasure as the Baron got out of the car, helped his Baroness out, kissed her with great satisfaction, and then led her up the steps to the open door. They surged forward then, uttering a wild welcome, shaking hands, exclaiming delightedly that of course they had known all along the Professor was safe.

Raf thanked them all in his calm way, then to Caspel: 'We shall take a stroll in the gardens, and perhaps tea in half an hour, Caspel,' then tucked Katrina's arm under his and went out of doors again.

'I must look awful,' said Katrina, lagging behind a little. 'I must do my face.'

'I like it like that,' declared Raf, 'covered in tears for me.' All the same, he paused long enough to mop them up for her with his handkerchief.

Caspel, Berthe and Nanny watched them strolling away to the shelter of the trees. Nanny spoke first. 'I knew it would be all right, I saw four magpies this morning.' Her Dutch was fluent but terrible.

'Magpies? What have magpies to do with it?' asked Caspel.

His companions gave him a pitying look. 'Four

for a boy,' they explained carefully, and smiled at each other, mentally getting out their knitting needles, infusing raspberry leaf tea and airing the christening robes stored so carefully in tissue paper.

Caspel looked down his old nose at them both. 'Tea in half an hour, the Baron said. It's a lovely afternoon for a stroll.'

Which was exactly what Raf was saying to his Kate, well away from the house by now and she wrapped securely in his arms, being kissed and loved and happy at last.

Harlequin understands...

the way you feel about love

Harlequin novels are stories of people in love—people like you— and all are beautiful romances, set in exotic faraway places.

Romance novels that speak
the language of love known to
women the world over.

Harlequin Presents...

A distinctive series of dramatic
love stories created
especially for you
by world-acclaimed
authors.

What readers say about Harlequin romance fiction...

"I feel as if I am in a different world every time I read a Harlequin."
A.T.* Detroit Michigan

"Harlequins have been my passport to the world. I have been many places without ever leaving my doorstep."
P.Z. Belvedere Illinois

"I like Harlequin books because they tell so much about other countries."
N.G. Rouyn, Quebec

"Your books offer a world of knowledge about places and people."
L.J. New Orleans, Louisiana

"Your books turn my...life into something quite exciting."
B.M.., Baldwin Park, California

"Harlequins take away the world's troubles and for a while you can live in a world of your own where love reigns supreme."

L.S. Beltsville Maryland

"Thank you for bringing romance back to me."

J.W. Tehachapi, California

"I find Harlequins are the only stories on the market that give me a satisfying romance with sufficient depth without being maudlin."

C.S. Bangor Maine

"Harlequins are magic carpets...away from pain and depression...away to other people and other countries one might never know otherwise."

H.R. Akron, Ohio

*Names available on request

Harlequin Romances

The books that let you escape
into the wonderful world of romance!
Trips to exotic places... interesting
plots... meeting memorable people...
the excitement of love.... These are
integral parts of Harlequin Romances—
the heartwarming novels read by
women everywhere.

Many early issues are now available.
Choose from this great selection!

Choose from this list of Harlequin Romance editions.*

Some of these book were originally published under different titles.